"I saw Scott Dillon

"You're kidding. How? Where? What did he say? Did he notice your gorgeous new look?" Hope grabbed Emily's shirt and pulled her toward the track. There were quite a few people running, even at six in the morning.

Emily started jogging. If you could call it that. "It wasn't pretty, Hope. I'd fallen flat on my rear in the middle of the hallway outside my classroom. He helped me up."

"Was it incredible? Did your eyes meet and—"

"I looked like death warmed over, and he didn't blink an eye."

They jogged in silence for a while. "I bet there was more. You probably just didn't see it."

Emily didn't argue. She wiped the sweat from her eyes, pulled up her sagging sweats and moved aside as she heard a runner approaching from behind.

"Hey!" the runner said as he reached her side. "Emily, I didn't know you ran."

Oh no.

Emily smiled at the man, with his windswept hair and perfectly muscled chest. *Perfect.*

Scott Dillon.

Dear Reader,

November is an exciting month here at Harlequin American Romance. You'll notice we have a brand-new look—but, of course, you can still count on Harlequin American Romance to bring you four terrific love stories sure to warm your heart.

Back by popular demand, Harlequin American Romance revisits the beloved town of Tyler, Wisconsin, in the RETURN TO TYLER series. Scandals, secrets and romances abound in this small town with fabulous stories written by some of your favorite authors. The always wonderful Jule McBride inaugurates this special four-book series with *Secret Baby Spencer*.

Bestselling author Muriel Jensen reprises her heartwarming WHO'S THE DADDY? series with *Father Fever*. Next, a former wallflower finally gets the attention of her high school crush when he returns to town and her friends give her a makeover and some special advice in *Catching His Eye*, the premiere of Jo Leigh's THE GIRLFRIENDS' GUIDE TO... continuing series. Finally, Harlequin American Romance's theme promotion, HAPPILY WEDDED AFTER, which focuses on marriages of convenience, continues with Pamela Bauer's *The Marriage Portrait*.

Enjoy them all—and don't forget to come back again next month when another installment in the RETURN TO TYLER series from Judy Christenberry is waiting for you.

Wishing you happy reading,

Melissa Jeglinski
Associate Senior Editor
Harlequin American Romance

CATCHING HIS EYE

Jo Leigh

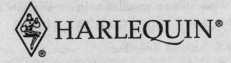

TORONTO • NEW YORK • LONDON
AMSTERDAM • PARIS • SYDNEY • HAMBURG
STOCKHOLM • ATHENS • TOKYO • MILAN • MADRID
PRAGUE • WARSAW • BUDAPEST • AUCKLAND

To Trysa, who lights the night with her smile.
Who holds us all in her heart.

ISBN 0-373-16851-9

CATCHING HIS EYE

Visit us at www.eHarlequin.com

Printed in U.S.A.

ABOUT THE AUTHOR

Jo Leigh currently lives just outside Las Vegas, Nevada, where she still can't get used to the slot machines in the grocery stores. Storytelling has always been a part of her life, whether as a producer in Hollywood, a screenwriter or a novelist. It probably began when she told her third grade teacher that elephants ate her homework.

Books by Jo Leigh

HARLEQUIN AMERICAN ROMANCE
695—QUICK, FIND A RING!
731—HUSBAND 101
736—DADDY 101
749—IF WISHES WERE...DADDIES
768—CAN'T RESIST A COWBOY
832—DOCTOR, DARLING
851—CATCHING HIS EYE*

*The Girlfriends' Guide To...

HARLEQUIN INTRIGUE
568—LITTLE GIRL FOUND

HARLEQUIN TEMPTATION
774—ONE WICKED NIGHT
799—SINGLE SHERIFF SEEKS...
827—TANGLED SHEETS
856—HOT AND BOTHERED

Don't miss any of our special offers. Write to us at the following address for information on our newest releases.

Harlequin Reader Service
U.S.: 3010 Walden Ave., P.O. Box 1325, Buffalo, NY 14269
Canadian: P.O. Box 609, Fort Erie, Ont. L2A 5X3

How To Catch A Man's Eye...
And Trade It In For His Heart!
Specially created for Emily Proctor by The Girlfriends

"Whatever you do, don't say yes on the first date!"
Samantha Barnett

"Be mysterious. Don't finish sentences.
Look off in the distance as if a faraway lover
is calling you. Let him wonder and make him wait."
Julia Carey

"For heaven's sake, go out and buy new underwear."
Lily Graham

"Don't play games. Just walk right up to him
and tell him every time you look at him you get all
hot and bothered. For once in your life, say yes!"
Hope Francis

"Take it slowly. Use your head.
It's too easy to make a mistake that will
cost you everything. This is serious."
Zoey Hoffman

"Help!"
Emily Proctor

Chapter One

The Girlfriends' Sixteenth Anniversary

Emily Proctor poured each of her girlfriends another frozen daiquiri. Midori daiquiris, to be precise. And, if one was getting picky about such things, they weren't really just girlfriends, they were The Girlfriends. Sworn to be there for each other through thick and thin. Together by choice, forged by sixteen years of school and parents and boyfriends and...oh, just *everything*.

"I shouldn't be drinking this," Lily said, but only after she'd taken a really big swallow. "I have to take JT to soccer at eight in the morning." She shuddered dramatically, making her impromptu ponytail wave back and forth. "The sitter can't. She's going to Dallas first thing tomorrow."

"Why don't you call Glen Cassidy...? He has to take Cody, so maybe he'll pick up JT, too."

Lily turned to Hope Francis. The polar opposite of Lily, Hope was five foot one to Lily's five foot seven, and Hope had dark hair, almost black. It was trimmed in a dramatic sort of pageboy. Really angular, though. On her, it worked. She looked exotic, especially with her Winona Ryder eyes, made smoky by the liberal use of black kohl and powder. Not to mention the fire-engine red lipstick, which was mostly on the rim of her glass. The problem with Hope, at least in her own eyes, was that she looked about seventeen, and it drove her insane.

Lily smiled broadly as she uncurled her legs and got up off the couch to follow up on that excellent advice. "That's why we keep you here, Hope. Because you're beautiful *and* brilliant."

Hope smiled demurely. Then she burped. Loudly.

Everyone cracked up as Emily crawled back on the hotel room bed and scrunched the pillow beneath her. It was so good to be together like this. All of them. Hope, Lily, Sam, Zoey and Julia. The Girlfriends.

They'd met in Mrs. Mann's fifth-grade class, at Sheridan elementary school. They'd bonded over their outrage at Paul Morrison's obnoxious game of pulling up their dresses on the playground.

Emily wondered for a moment what had happened to Paul. But that wasn't important. What was important was that the six of them had come together like pieces of a puzzle. They'd all *fit*.

As she sipped her drink, Zoey turned the topic to her hair, as she did every year, complaining that it was too red, too curly, too hideous to be shown in public. It was utter nonsense, and the rest of the girls told her so. Every year.

"It's wonderful hair," Samantha said. "Very Nicole Kidman."

Zoey sighed. "Yeah. Wouldn't it be nice if I also had her body? And her face?"

Julia smiled wryly. "It would be even nicer if you had her husband."

Zoey, who was sprawled in the chair across from the couch, turned to Julia. "Oh, really? You like him?"

"What's not to like? That smile. Those eyes. That tight little behind…"

"He's too short," Lily said, coming back from her phone call to plop down on the couch again. "I like them tall. Tall and strong and kinda wiry."

"No kidding?" Julia said, but Emily and everyone else in the room knew she was being sarcastic. Lily had always been specific about the man she was going to marry. Although she never admitted it, her perfect man was one Jesse Hyatt, who had been in high school with them. He'd never given Lily the time of day, unfortunately, but she still considered him the epitome of masculine perfection.

"I," Lily said, sniffing her displeasure, "have certain standards, which some of you are sadly lacking."

A great hue and cry came from the floor, the couch, the chair, the bed. Emily laughed. "Oh, please! This from a woman who got knocked up at age sixteen?''

''JT is the best thing that's ever happened to me,'' Lily said, and from her tone, Emily realized she needed to back off. Most of the time Lily joked with the rest of them about her unorthodox family, but sometimes, like when she'd had a little too much to drink, she could get pretty defensive.

''Sorry, kiddo.'' Emily stood up so she could get some cookies. They'd each brought food for the weekend, and as far as Emily could tell, there wasn't one nutrient in the bunch. They'd concentrated on the three basic food groups: chocolate, chips and cream filling.

Julia snorted in a most unfeminine manner. ''Maybe we'd believe you had this non Jesse Hyatt ideal if you'd actually go out on a date. I've got news for you. You can't get your virginity back, no matter how long you hold out.''

''I'm not holding out,'' Lily said. ''I just haven't met the right man yet.''

''At least you're not alone,'' Hope said with a sigh. ''You'd think one of us would have found Mr. Right by now, wouldn't you?''

Zoey nodded. ''Or at the very least, Mr. Okay.''

Sam shook her head. ''I know you're kidding, Zoey. You must be. Finding a life partner is the most important decision in a woman's life. It's not to be taken lightly.''

Hope grinned at Emily. ''Too bad Sam's ideal man is too old for her. And he's married.''

''Who might that be?'' Sam asked, raising her perfectly arched eyebrows.

''Bob Villa, of course. Between the two of you, there wouldn't be a single store-bought item in your house. You'd knit the couches, he'd build the stove. You're perfect for each other.''

Sam sighed. ''Just because I'm handy—''

''Handy? You out-Martha Stewart Martha Stewart.''

''Look who's talking, Ms. Everything-Has-To-Match Hope.''

''Hey!'' Emily put her hands on her hips, but instead of giving her friends the stern talking-to they deserved, she noticed that of all the women in the room, hers were the only hips that were large, economy-size. It was depressing.

Hope, Lily and Samantha were the perfect width for their height. Julia was too skinny, despite the fact that she ate like a little oinker, darn it. And Zoey was just plain voluptuous, even though she thought she was fat. She wasn't. But Emily was.

Not life-threateningly fat, but she could lose a good twenty or twenty-five pounds. She *should* lose—

''Emily?'' Hope said, interrupting her thoughts.

''Yes?''

''Weren't you supposed to be yelling at us?''

''Oh, yeah. Stop it.''

The girls cracked up again, and things were the way they should be once more, only Emily had to force her smile. Couldn't she go one blessed weekend without obsessing about her weight?

Of course not. Especially after the news she'd heard just this morning. She might as well tell them now. But first, she needed one more cookie before she sat down.

As Emily reached for the bag Lily poured herself another daiquiri.

"I suppose that means you don't have to take JT tomorrow?" Zoey asked, eyeing the full glass of sweet, cold booze.

"Nope. I can get as toasted as I want."

"Which isn't going to be all that toasted," Sam said. "There will be no throwing up tonight. We're too old for that nonsense."

"Yeah," Hope agreed. "Hangovers have completely lost their charm."

"I've got an announcement," Emily said. But she must have said it very softly, because no one looked at her. She cleared her throat and tried again. "I've got an announcement!"

That quieted the room. All eyes were upon her, and she felt her face heat up. She hated blushing, but that was yet another thing she had no control over.

"Well?" Sam said.

"Scott Dillon is coming back to town."

Silence.

A really long stretch of silence.

Hope looked at Sam. Lily looked at Julia. Zoey looked at Emily, then looked away.

"When?" Lily asked.

"Oh, um, tomorrow."

"What!" shouted the chorus.

"I'm fine," Emily assured them. "It's no big deal."

"My behind," Zoey said, bounding to her feet. "Why did you wait so long to say anything?"

"I just found out."

"In the last five seconds?"

"No. This morning."

Zoey grabbed a small water bottle from the side table then settled her gaze on Emily. "What's the story?"

"Kelly told me, since his father died, Scott's mom is having a tough time running the store. So Scott's coming home to help until they figure out what to do."

"Kelly?" Hope turned to Lily. "Isn't she Jeff Whaley's girlfriend?"

"Yeah. She's the one that got that boob job."

Julia shook her head at the two gossips. "That's not the main item on the agenda, ladies."

The miscreants focused on Emily. She wished they'd go on talking about boob jobs. Scott Dillon wasn't her favorite topic, outside of her daydreams, that is. But at least she didn't have to go into any lengthy explanations. They all knew she'd been crazy about him since tenth grade. That he'd played Romeo to her Juliet in drama class, which turned the crush into mad, passionate love. And that he'd broken her heart when he'd taken Cathy Turner to the prom.

Her friends even had the decency not to mention that she'd never stood a chance with Scott. A gorgeous guy like him, football captain, president of the class, would never consider a girl like her in a romantic sense. That was not the way the world worked. She was the friend, the sounding board, the one who'd find out if the Cathy Turners of the world were interested in the Scott Dillons. But she'd never be the date. The love interest. Not with her chubby cheeks and her large economy-size hips.

"So, are you going to do something about it?" Zoey asked.

"Like what?"

"Like ask him out."

Emily burst out laughing. "Yeah, right."

"I'm not kidding. He's always liked you, Emily. I mean he still calls you, right?"

"Once. He called once a hundred years ago. As a friend. Nothing more."

"He's older now. More mature."

"And dating older, more mature supermodels. Not one chance in hell he'd ever go for me that way."

"You don't know that."

Emily lifted her right brow.

Zoey's shoulders sagged. "It could happen," she said weakly.

''No, it couldn't,'' Emily said with a sigh. ''But it sure would have been nice, huh?''

''What?''

''One night. One perfect night. Champagne, a full moon, music, flowers. I would have been happy with that, you know? With the memory.''

No one spoke for a moment and, just as startling, no one ate anything for a moment. Emily guessed they were all thinking of their own secret dreams. Those heartfelt wishes for things that could never be.

She'd be fine. She would. She was a champ at landing on her feet. ''Okay,'' she said, climbing off the bed again, more than ready to change the subject. ''I say we all get into our jammies and start some serious gossip.''

''Huh?''

''Shh.''

Sam blinked, trying to make sense of what she was hearing. It was too dark to see, and what the—

''Come on,'' Hope whispered. ''And don't make any noise.''

Sam threw back her covers and climbed out of the cot she'd won playing Rock, Paper, Scissors. It wasn't the bed, but it wasn't the floor, either. She followed Hope toward the bathroom, and when she saw that it was nearly four in the morning, she almost turned right around and went back to bed.

Hope anticipated the move, however, and

grabbed her hand, pulling her toward whatever the heck was going on.

They reached the bathroom, and Hope shoved Sam inside, then Hope joined her. Once the door was closed, the light came on. Everyone was there. Except Emily.

Zoey had on her Bugs Bunny pajamas. Lily wore a nightshirt that advertised a Stephen King novel. Julia had on a cropped T-shirt that showed off her perfectly flat tummy and boxers that showed off her perfectly gorgeous legs. And Hope? She had on men's pajamas. Both the top and bottom. Sam's conservative white nightgown seemed hideously dull.

"Okay, so here's what I propose," Hope said, hopping up on the sink counter with far too much energy for four a.m. "I say we give Emily what she wants."

"A good night's sleep?" Zoey suggested.

Hope gave her a look. "No. One night with Scott Dillon. One perfect night."

Sam's mouth hung open, and she wasn't alone in her bewilderment. All the girlfriends except Hope, of course, looked stunned.

"Are you nuts?" Lily asked.

Zoey nodded. "She'd kill us."

Julia sat down on the commode seat. "What are we supposed to do? Hypnotize him into dating her? Buy him for her?"

Hope smiled. "I don't think it will come to that.

I think, if we do our jobs correctly, Scott Dillon will ask Emily Proctor out of his own accord.''

"And why would he," Lily asked, "when he's never been interested in her before?"

"Because we're going to take our little Emily, and turn her into the sexiest, most gorgeous creature he's ever laid eyes on. That's why."

No one spoke. Someone, Zoey probably, hiccuped. They exchanged glances. Finally Hope threw her arms into the air, accidentally sending Emily's toothbrush flying into the bathtub. "Well? Are we or are we not The Girlfriends?"

"We are," Zoey said.

"And do we or don't we help one another?"

"We do," Sam agreed. "But—"

"But nothing." Hope leaned forward. "We can do this, guys. And you know what's going to happen? Emily's going to come away from this with so much self-confidence, with so much pride, that she'll be able to get any man she wants. Scott Dillon, George Clooney. Whoever."

"Little optimistic there, aren't you, Hope?" Julia asked.

Hope nodded. "I'd agree if it was just me working on Emily. But it's *us*. All of us. We can do this, guys. I just know we can."

Julia waved her hand. "One more thing? What if Emily says no?"

Hope jumped down from the sink. "Then we'll make her say yes."

THE FOOTBALL TROPHIES WERE lined up in perfect symmetry, polished to a high sheen, exactly where they'd been nine years ago when he'd moved out of his parents' home to go to Texas A&M.

Scott shifted his attention to the wall, to the pictures, the green and white flags, the display of Sheridan High memorabilia his parents had preserved like a shrine. They had been good days. Important days. But he'd moved on. At least, he'd tried.

He turned back to his open suitcase and started putting his clothes in the bureau, guilt eating a hole inside him. He didn't want to be here. He was on the cusp, inches away from a dream career after years of disappointment. Destined, finally, to regain his former glory. But instead of preparing for an interview at ESPN, he was in his old bedroom, in his old town, in his old life.

It wasn't fair. But, as Coach Teller always said, nothing's fair except a fine spring day. Coach. At least Scott would get to visit him. That was a good thing.

He heard his mother in the hallway, her slippers scratching lightly on the hardwood floor. "Scott?"

"Yes, Mom?" He shut the top drawer, pasted on a smile and turned to face her. God, she'd gotten old. Old beyond her years. It was frightening.

He'd been born late in his folks' lives, when his mother had been forty-one and his father forty-five. His mother had always had more energy than any two people he knew, but now she walked with a shuffle. It took her a long time to climb the stairs. She'd stopped coloring her hair, so it was white now, instead of the strawberry-blonde it had been forever. The vibrant part of her had gone, and he wanted more than anything else to help her get it back.

The decline had started when his father died. She'd loved the old man, and Scott had a feeling she wanted to join him. But she wouldn't. Not while she had her son to care for.

"I've made cabbage rolls for dinner," she said.

"Ah, Mom, you spoil me."

She smiled, and the wrinkles around her eyes made it hard for him to keep his own grin in place. How could he leave her to fend for herself?

"Do you have everything you need?"

He nodded. "It's just like it always was."

"It's home," she said. "It'll always be your home. You know that, don't you?"

His mother hadn't ever been a big woman, but she'd shrunk somehow over the years, so when he hugged her, the top of her head came only to his chin. He held her cautiously, afraid to squeeze too hard for fear she'd break. She'd lost too much weight. Her little arms went around his waist, and for a long moment, they rocked each other.

Scott knew without doubt that he was responsible for this woman, just as she'd been responsible for him for all his growing-up years. She wouldn't sell the store, and she couldn't run the store, so that left him.

Instead of being the newest ESPN sports commentator at the unheard-of age of twenty-six, he was going to be the manager of Dillon's Market.

Nothing was fair except a fine spring day.

"ARE YOU *INSANE?*"

Hope shook her head. "Come on, Emily. You know you want to."

"I do not!" She hopped off the bed and grabbed her clothes, anxious to get out of her nightgown and end this conversation.

"You do so," Hope said, following her across the hotel room to the bathroom. "It'll be a great adventure. And face it, girl, you need an adventure."

"An adventure in humiliation? No, thank you."

"Who said anything about humiliation?"

Emily couldn't believe her friend was so dense. Actually, Hope was such a dreamer, it made sense she couldn't see the downside of her little scheme. But Lily had both feet firmly on the ground. Sam had been the most practical person in Sheridan, and now that she'd moved, she was probably the most practical person in San Francisco, too. Zoey had some flights of fancy from time to time, but surely she could see this was a disaster waiting to happen.

"I'm going to take a shower," Emily said. "And when I get out, I don't want to discuss this again. *Capiche?*"

Hope opened her mouth, but Emily didn't stick around to hear her argument. She went into the

bathroom and locked the door behind her. Of all
the nutty...

She put her fresh clothes on the counter, turned
on the water in the shower, and then she blew it.
She took off her nightgown and saw herself in the
mirror.

Oh, God.

It wasn't that she was hideous. It was that she
was so *plain.* Nondescript brown hair. Eyes that
were a dull shade of brown. Of course, the double
chin did wonders for her face. The rest of her? Five
feet four inches short and damn near one hundred
and sixty. She wanted to cry.

Instead, she banished her own image from her
memory and climbed into the shower. Washing oc-
cupied her mind for a while, but if she didn't cool
it she'd have no skin left. She stopped her feverish
scrubbing and surrendered to the water. With
closed eyes, she relaxed her shoulders, unclenched
her hands.

They thought they could make her over. Trans-
form her like Cinderella the night of the ball. But
she knew better. She didn't have what it took to
be beautiful. Even if she lost all the weight and
got new makeup and clothes, she'd still be plain
old Emily Proctor. And Emily Proctor didn't get
to have Scott Dillon.

So why bother?

She held her breath for a moment, steadied herself with a hand on the cold wall. For the first time
ever, she actually realized what she'd just said.

Why bother? If she couldn't have Scott Dillon, *why bother?* Oh, God. She was the one who was insane, not her friends. What kind of a life choice was that? Wasn't *she* worth bothering for? Just for being here? For being *her?*

No. The answer to that had been no her whole life. Because she couldn't be as pretty as Julia, or as stylish and witty as Hope or as classy as Sam or as brilliant as Zoey, or as brave as Lily, she'd thrown in the towel on her own life.

Coward! That's what she was. A big, yellow coward. Hiding out in the only place she'd ever lived, sneaking pieces of chocolate instead of feasting at the banquet of life.

She'd lost the game before it had begun.

So what if she'd never get Scott Dillon. If she didn't do something about her life, she'd never be Emily Proctor. Not the Emily Proctor she was supposed to be.

At twenty-six, she had no idea who that was supposed to be. High school teacher? Yes, but that shouldn't be all of who she was. Drama teacher? Again, that wasn't enough. Friend. Yes. Yes, that one was very important. Daughter? Of course. But every definition she came up with was about something outside of herself.

Who was she? Right now, standing naked in the shower at the Sheridan Holiday Inn?

Tears welled only to be washed away, leaving no trace. Her fate would too, if she didn't do something about it.

And the something closest at hand was as Hope put it, the Scott Dillon Diet, Exercise and Beauty Regimen. With emotional, physical and spiritual help from The Girlfriends.

It would mean no more French fries in the car. No more ice cream in the middle of the night. It would mean exercising, and sticking to it even when it was uncomfortable. She'd actually have to acknowledge her body, her lifestyle, her loneliness.

Something funny happened in her stomach. Fear, but not just fear. Excitement. That was it. She actually felt excited.

Maybe she couldn't have Scott, but she could have a life. And maybe, if she learned to respect and love herself, she'd be ready to have someone else love her, too.

She turned off the shower and grabbed a towel from the rack. This was it. Her last chance to change her mind. If she told the gang she was in, they'd never let her alone about it. They were nothing if not persistent.

Stepping out onto the bath mat, she looked at the mirror, but all she saw was fog. Moving closer, she rubbed out a large clear circle. It was time to say goodbye. To all the old comforts. To the familiar pain.

She waved, and then the fog crept back and she wasn't there anymore.

Chapter Two

The lunch bell rang, and twenty-one copies of *Romeo and Juliet* slammed shut at the same time. It was no use going on. Her fourth-period senior English class had already gone to lunch, even though they waited, albeit impatiently, for her to give the homework assignment and excuse them.

"Read pages eighteen through thirty, and write two pages about the relationship between the Montegues and the Capulets."

A collective groan almost obscured the scraping of chairs as her students rushed to escape. But today Emily didn't care. She had her own agenda.

Day four of the regimen had started out badly. Because she was a fool, she'd started her exercise program with far too much vigor, and her muscles, particularly her leg muscles, were proving her folly.

She winced as she erased the blackboard, cursing her own stupidity. Why had she ever agreed to this cockamamy scheme? It was dumb, it hurt, and she didn't want to play anymore.

She wouldn't tell the others, though. Not yet. There was plenty of time to disappoint her friends.

And herself.

Damn. There went a perfectly good opportunity to quit. Now she'd have to eat her salad with balsamic vinegar dressing, no oil. She'd have to drink her eight ounces of water. She'd have to keep her word.

But she didn't have to like it.

It took her ten minutes to gather her things and straighten up the classroom. Unfortunately, she had papers, lots of them, to correct. But after lunch, she had drama, and she didn't want to lug her things around. Since the auditorium was right there at the parking lot she'd put her stuff in the car, and after sixth period, she'd be out of here.

By the time she'd picked up everything she needed, her arms were full and her muscles protested in a most vivid way. But she went into the hall, lined with lockers and kids and banners announcing the upcoming football game. She put all her things down so she could lock the door, then picked them up again. She headed toward the door, the parking lot, wondering if she was too young to use Ben-Gay.

She heard the accident seconds before it even happened. Tennis shoes slapped the linoleum.

Rushed at her like a freight train. But it was too late to get out of the way and she squeezed her eyes shut as she was hit broadside.

Her book bag flew out of her hands. She struggled to keep her balance, but there was no way. She fell hard, landing on her right hip.

The kid, someone she didn't recognize, didn't even stop to say he was sorry. He just ran like hell to the end of the hall, and exited, stage right.

Gretchen Foley stared at her from in front of her locker. "Are you all right, Ms. Proctor?"

"Yes, Gretchen. I'm fine."

"Should I go get the nurse or something?"

"That won't be necessary."

Gretchen nodded and headed toward the cafeteria. She didn't even bother to pick up a single piece of paper. What was it with kids today? Had they all been raised by wolves?

Just then, a masculine hand came out of nowhere, extended in front of her. She sighed, glad that at least one student on campus had some manners.

She looked up at her Lochinvar, and her heart froze. Scott Dillon. Oh, God! Anyone but him! She'd gone out of her way to avoid him. She didn't want him to see her like this. Especially not like *this!*

He frowned, making his perfect dark brows come close together. "Are you really all right?"

She nodded, unable to speak.

He glanced at his hand, and she took hold of him, praying she wouldn't give him a hernia as he helped her up. To her utter relief, he didn't strain himself at all.

"Hey!" he said. "I didn't know it was you."

"It's me."

"Well, how do you like that. What are you doing here?"

"I work here."

"Right. That's right. I remember." He shook his head and she wasn't sure if it was because she was still living in Sheridan, or because she had come to teach at their alma mater. But he didn't stay perplexed for long. Instead, he started picking up her books and papers.

"It's great to see you. How you doing, Emily?"

"I'm fine, Scott," she said, lying through her teeth. "You're looking well." And he was. Oh, mama. He was more beautiful than ever. He towered over her at well over six feet. His dark, wavy hair was slightly unkempt, and he looked devilishly handsome. Dark chocolate eyes sparkled behind sinfully long lashes. And that smile. She'd been a sucker for that smile since day one.

He waved away her compliment, handed her the last of her papers, then glanced down the hall. "I'm supposed to meet Coach for lunch. I'm late."

"Go. Go on."

"But you need help with your books."

"I can handle it. Honestly. Now go. I know Coach hates it when anyone's late. It was good to see you again."

"Yeah. We'll have to get together for coffee or something."

She nodded, but he didn't see. He'd already started down the hall. Down the very same hall where she'd watched him, five days a week, and loved him from afar. Where he'd kissed Cathy Turner, blissfully unaware that he'd broken her heart.

Her smile died. She had to congratulate herself. She'd sounded perfectly normal. Perfectly calm. Despite the turmoil swirling inside. He'd seen her at her worst. Splayed on the floor like some giant amoeba, arms and legs akimbo, hair a horror, and she'd even managed to lose one shoe.

Perfect. A fairy-tale reunion if she'd ever seen one. She'd managed to blow it before it had even begun—

Wait.

This wasn't about Scott, right? The sudden urge for fast food might be about him, but her determination not to give in was hers and hers alone.

So he'd seen her. So what? It was bound to happen. So it wasn't in the most flattering light. Big deal. The truth was, they'd been friends, once. Good friends. They'd talked about their dreams for a shining future. Shared their fears and laughter as they sat in the last row of the auditorium waiting for their turn on the stage. Despite her crush, she'd liked Scott. She'd never understood what he saw in Cathy, but hey, who knows? Maybe Cathy had hidden depth. Really well-hidden. But that was neither here nor there. What was relevant now was Emily's desire to go the distance. To be the best she could be.

It was time to eat her salad. With balsamic vinegar, no oil.

SCOTT HURRIED DOWN the familiar halls, wishing he'd come earlier so that he could have lingered, savored his memories. But as Emily said, Coach hated to be kept waiting.

Emily Proctor.

He hadn't expected to see her again. It surprised him that she'd stayed in Sheridan. She was so bright, he imagined her in New York or something, writing books or in politics. She'd be a good teacher, though. Her students were lucky.

He'd thought about her from time to time. About their talks, mostly. About how he'd looked forward to his classes with her. He'd taken out his yearbook once and seeing her picture was like a dose of medicine. She'd been a better friend in high school than he'd understood at the time. He regretted not keeping in touch with her.

As he passed the lockers, the pep-rally posters and the students with their backpacks and cell phones, the smell of the place brought him back to his own days here. Funny about that smell. He hadn't noticed it back then, but when he'd walked through the front doors a few minutes ago, it had hit him hard. The combination of young, sweaty bodies, perfume, old gym socks, books, chalk… It was the smell of his youth, of his heyday. A damn fine smell.

And then to bump into Emily? That really took him back. She'd been so easy to talk to. So funny. She'd had those long bangs. He remembered wondering how she saw with all that hair in her eyes. And she was always hanging out with her girlfriends. Giggling, passing notes, getting into the kind of trouble that got stern looks from teachers. Nothing more. Innocent. But then, hadn't they all been innocent back then?

Yeah. Emily Proctor. She'd been great. A good friend. Maybe she could be his friend, again. It didn't look like he was leaving anytime soon. The store was a mess and needed someone in charge. There wasn't anyone standing in the wings. The job was his whether he wanted it or not.

He pushed open the door to the quad and set out for the gym. The trees seemed bigger, the grass scragglier, but the biggest change he noticed was the students. They looked so young! At twenty-six he'd never thought much about his age, but now the truth hit him that he wasn't the hotshot he used to be. That star had tarnished with the snap of his right ankle. Every year, new and better players made first string, and the one thing that would have made Scott special, the chance to be ESPN's youngest sports commentator ever, had slipped through his fingers like so much sand.

His gait slowed as he passed the science building. He wished he could just go. Cut out with no regrets, go to Bristol and take that interview. But he couldn't. He wouldn't be able to live with himself if he did.

So the next best thing was to get the hell over it. Get on with the life he had, instead of dreaming about the life he was supposed to have.

A dose of Coach was exactly what he needed.

THE GRASS WAS STILL WET, which added insult to injury. No one should be up at this hour, let alone doing sit-ups in the grassy middle of the high school track field.

Only three more to go.

Emily glared at Hope, which was pretty easy to do considering Hope was currently sitting on Emily's feet while she did her sit-ups. What Hope didn't know was that her life was spared only by the fact that Emily wasn't strong enough to knock her down.

"Come on, Emily. You can do it."

"Go—" Emily forced her aching abs to lift her to a sitting position. "To—" She touched her elbows to her knees, and started a slow ascent back to position one. But instead of keeping her head an inch from the floor, she collapsed. "Hell," she said breathlessly, but proud she'd made the effort.

"Come on, you wussie girl. You weak-assed lazy bones. Two more!"

She tried. And failed. Her groan echoed off the empty bleachers. "I'll give you a hundred dollars to go away."

Hope laughed. "Your money's no good here, missy. I want to see another sit-up and I want to see it now!"

"Then go rent *An Officer and a Gentleman*. But first, get off me."

Hope sighed heavily as she moved over. "Pitiful."

"Let's see you do twenty sit-ups."

"If I had time, I'd do exactly that."

"You lie like a rug," Emily said, rubbing her stomach and feeling quite sorry for herself.

"Hey! I do ten pull-ups and twenty push-ups every day."

"You do not."

"I *could* do them. If I woke up in time."

Emily rolled her eyes. "Yeah, well, if I had a brother, he'd like cheese."

"What?"

"Never mind. Just help me up."

Hope jumped up sprightly, then held her hand out. Emily grabbed it, much as she had grabbed Scott's hand two days ago.

"I saw him, you know," Emily said.

"Pardon?"

"I said, I saw him."

"Him who?"

Emily sighed. "Scott Dillon. Remember him? The point of all this torture?"

"Oh, *him.* You're kidding. How? Where? What did he say?"

"I have to go shower."

"Oh, no. You're not leaving. You're coming with me. We're doing two laps around the track before we finish."

"What do you mean, we? I'm not doing any such thing."

Hope grabbed her by the T-shirt and pulled her toward the high school track. There were quite a few people jogging already, even though it was only just past six in the morning, on a Saturday no less. Some teachers, but mostly students circled the infield, almost every one of them looking tan and fit and wonderful in their little teeny shorts. Not her. No one laid eyes on her thighs. Ever.

She started jogging, if you could call it that. It

was more a lumbering walk, actually. But Hope let go of her shirt, so that was something.

"So, tell me. Damn, girl, you sure do know how to build the suspense."

"It wasn't pretty, Hope."

"Huh?"

"I was flat on my butt in the middle of the hall-way outside my classroom."

Hope stopped. Emily jogged past her. Slowly.

"Oh, no."

"Oh, yes."

"Why were you on the floor?"

"Doing yoga." She was too tired for sarcasm. After gulping a few breaths, she slowed her pace a wee bit. "Some kid, and I think it might have been Tommy Wells, crashed into me, and I fell."

"And?"

"And Scott helped me up."

"Was it incredible? Did your eyes meet and—"

"It was humiliating. I looked like death warmed over and he didn't blink an eye."

"He didn't remember you?"

"Yes, he did. But it was nothing. A big fat zero."

"Are you sure?"

"I was there."

"Oh."

They jogged in silence for a while. Emily might

have said more, but her lungs were preoccupied with trying to save her life.

"I bet there was more. You probably just didn't see it."

"There was no more."

"I don't believe it."

Emily didn't argue with her. But she did move to the right as she heard an approaching runner. She also wiped the sweat from her eyes and pulled up her sagging sweats.

"Hey!" the runner said as he got to her side.

Oh, God.

"Emily! I didn't know you ran."

She smiled at Scott, who looked like he should have been on a box of Wheaties with his perfect chest and windswept hair. She thought about her own hair, elegantly swathed in a decrepit sweatband, with just a few insouciant tendrils plastered against her cheek. About the shirt she had so carefully chosen this morning, emblazoned with Bart Simpson shouting "Don't Have a Cow!"

"Hey, Scott," Hope said, looking far too pretty.

"Hope? Oh, man, this is old home week. You're still here, too?"

"I ask myself why every morning, but yes, I'm still here.

He laughed as he slowed down to meet Emily's pace, and try as she might she couldn't improve it. It was probably better to go slow than to actually have a heart attack at the next quarter-mile. On the other hand...

"So what about that cup of coffee we talked about the other day?" he asked.

She nodded, not sure if she could continue to jog and speak at the same time.

"Great. How about tomorrow. You don't work on Sunday, do you?"

She shook her head this time.

"I'll have to," he said, "but I can take a break around four if that works for you."

Again she nodded. This time throwing in a smile.

"Great. I'll call you. You're in the book?"

More nodding.

"Okay, then." He turned to Hope. "Great seeing you again."

"Yeah," she said, her voice as even as his. "Nice to have you back."

"Have a good run," he said, then he put on some speed, leaving her and Hope in the dust.

At least he gave Emily something terrific to look at as he raced away. She kept moving her legs, swinging her arms, all the while looking for an escape plan. At the next curve in the track, she headed for the girls' locker room, and she didn't stop until she was safely inside.

She made her way to a bench and collapsed, her

lungs burning like fire, her legs like Jell-O, her face so hot she could fry an egg on her forehead.

The door slammed and Hope found her still gasping for breath.

"Oh, my God!" she said. "What are the odds? But hey, he asked you out. That's something. That's incredible."

Emily looked up into Hope's beautiful, sweat-free face. "What the hell are you talking about?"

"Tomorrow. I heard him ask you. And you said yes."

"For the record, I said nothing. There's no way I'm going to coffee with him tomorrow."

Hope sat down on the other side of the bench. "Emily—"

"Don't start. Don't quibble. Just know that I quit. Right here, right now. It was a stupid idea."

"Gee, thanks."

"You know what I mean."

"Yeah, I do. But what I don't understand is why you want to quit."

"You were right there!"

"Where?"

"Don't be dense, Hope. He thinks I'm his buddy from English lit. He'll never see me any other way."

"You don't know that."

Emily gave her a look, but she didn't argue. In fact, all her arguments ended right then. Except...

"It's completely unacceptable. You're going to see him if I have to drag you to the coffee shop by your hair."

"You and what army?"

"Lily, Sam, Zoey, Julia—"

"Sam and Zoey aren't even in town."

"They'll fly in for the occasion."

Emily let go a troubled sigh. She'd had such dreams about meeting Scott. How she'd look, her hair, her nails. How cool she'd be, sophisticated enough to sit next to Dorothy at the Algonquin. She'd imagined his reaction dozens of times. His eyes widening, his jaw slackening. His inability to string three words together. It was supposed to have been heaven. A meeting so gorgeous songs would be written about it.

Instead, she'd sweated and gasped, panted like a dog. She could have gotten over the incident in the school hallway. But now she was two strikes down. She wasn't anxious to go up to bat again.

"Are you listening to me?" Hope asked.

Not only had Emily not been listening, she hadn't even seen Hope get up and take her shirt off. Her dark hair was a mess, but it still managed to look sexy and sleek. Hope, who considered her looks average, who thought that she was too short and her nose too big, wasn't any of those things. She was beautiful. Everyone saw it but her.

"Why do we do this to ourselves?" Emily asked, surprised that she'd said it aloud.

"What?"

"Think of ourselves in the worst possible light."

Hope grabbed her T-shirt and pulled it on, then came back to the bench. "I don't know. We do, though, don't we?"

"All the time. It's never about how happy we are with our eyes, but how miserable we are with our nose."

Hope nodded. "Men don't do that."

"I'll say. They think if they can stand upright they're hot stuff."

"So go see him, Em. Why not?"

Emily met her gaze. "I don't know."

"I do. Go. Go with no expectations except to see an old friend. Go without making yourself nuts, just like you were meeting one of us. Go and talk to him, and let him see who you are now. The very worst that's going to happen is you'll have a new friend."

She nodded. "Okay. Why not? I'll go, and I'll talk and I'll leave my expectations at home."

Chapter Three

Scott handed Mrs. Newberry her package of green beans then forced a smile. The immediate reward of a return smile did little to elevate his mood. He couldn't stop thinking about the plane tickets sitting in his suitcase. First class, round trip from Los Angeles to Bristol, Connecticut. The plane would be in the air right now, with some other passenger in his seat.

"Are the tomatoes ripe?" a strident voice said from behind him.

He turned to find Dora Weeks, one of his mother's closest friends. She was his mother's age, but right now, she looked years younger. She was a tiny thing, not even five feet tall, with completely white close-cropped hair. The biggest thing about her were her glasses, which were so thick they made her eyes look twice their size.

"Yes, Mrs. Weeks, they're ripe."

"Not too ripe."

"No. In fact, if you'd like I can help you pick one out."

She nodded. "Your father always picked out my tomatoes."

"He was good at that," Scott said, an unexpected twinge hitting his heart.

"That's right." Mrs. Weeks followed him toward the produce department, forcing him to slow his walk to a crawl. "He knew his vegetables."

"He also taught me, Mrs. Weeks." They passed the bread aisle, and Scott noticed the stock was low. Of course that meant he had to fix it, because there was no stock boy anymore. Not for a month. His mother hadn't even tried to hire a new one.

He finally reached the tomatoes, and he looked for a beauty. All the produce was good, that hadn't changed, but there were tomatoes and there were *tomatoes*.

He sniffed a contender, searching for a distinct aroma he knew intimately but couldn't describe. Years of working part-time and summers in the store under his father's watchful gaze had made Scott a grocer, whether he liked it or not.

"Your mother must be so proud."

"Thank you. I had a good run, before the old ankle blew."

Mrs. Weeks looked up at him, her huge Mr. Magoo eyes confused. "A good run? I meant she must be so proud that you came home. That you're here when she needs you. She's not well, you know. She tries to hide it, but I can tell.''

Plane tickets flashed in his mind for a second, but he chased them away. If he started down that path, he'd never find his way back. ''I know, Mrs. Weeks, and I'm very grateful you watch out for her.''

''I do my best.''

He presented his tomato on his open palm. ''Here she is. Best tomato in the place.''

Mrs. Weeks smiled as she took the vegetable in her hands. She smelled it and smiled. ''Like father like son.''

I hope not. The uncharitable thought caught him off guard. What a thing to think. His father had been a fine man. Honest and thorough and kind, even though he was tough. He'd worked his whole life so that the family would have a decent house and cars, and so that Scott could go to college.

''You tell Mary I'll come by on Tuesday.''

''I will, Mrs. Weeks.''

She headed toward the checkout counter. He wondered if her daughter came to visit. Probably. Probably called all the time. Franny Weeks was eleven years older than him, and she used to be his baby-sitter. She'd been a piece of work. Always had her nose in a book. Hated sports, even watching them.

He headed toward the bread aisle to see what he

had to bring from the back. For nine-thirty on a Sunday morning, there were quite a few people in the small store. Neighbors, each one.

He noticed Jack Gates, who had retired after a lifetime of working at the hardware store. Scott remembered when Jack had helped him build a doghouse for Knute, Scott's old mutt. Knute had passed on fifteen years ago, but the doghouse, still in the backyard, looked weathered but sturdy. Just like Jack himself.

Aura Lee Merchant studied the salad dressing, her body shaking with Parkinson's disease. She'd been a teacher at Sheridan Elementary, although he hadn't been in her class.

Ted Cooper, Mrs. Freed, Karen Crane. They'd all been coming here for years. No superstores for them. They liked the personal service, but more, they liked the continuity. At least that was his theory.

But whatever the reason they liked the store, they would stop coming if things didn't improve. The rolls were almost all gone. Half the name brand breads were gone, too. He'd better call the distributors and find out what was going on.

A young man, surprising in this store of older customers, approached him tentatively. "Mr. Dillon?"

"Yep."

The boy cleared his throat. Wiped his hands on

his jeans. He looked to Scott to be about thirteen. His Cowboys T-shirt had seen better days, but it was clean. "I'm Jeff Grogin."

"How you doing?"

Jeff thrust out his hand. Scott shook it, wondering if this was his next stock boy.

"Is it true that during the state championships you threw for 549 yards?"

A fan. Too young to have seen Scott play. But in a town this size, his football career was as well-known as the Pledge of Allegiance. "Yep. It's true."

The boy blinked a couple of times. "I play some football, too."

"Do you?"

"For the Tigers. I'm the varsity quarterback."

"How old are you?"

"Seventeen, sir."

Sir. Suddenly Scott felt like he was a hundred. "Well, what can I do for you?"

"I was wondering if you'd like to, um maybe have a Coke or something?"

Scott raised his eyebrow. "Are you asking me out on a date?"

Bobby's face flushed scarlet. "No! I mean, no, sir. I just thought—"

Scott waved away the boy's explanation and smiled to show he'd been kidding. "I know what you mean. Sure, sure. We can do that. Just not today.''

''Anytime, sir.''

''But we can't go if you keep calling me sir. Got it?''

''Yes, sir. I mean—''

''Scott. Scott is the name you're looking for.''

The boy, who Scott still couldn't believe was old enough to play football, grinned like he'd just won a new car. ''Great. Maybe tomorrow? Or Tuesday. Tuesday would be just fine.''

''You seem to have some free time on your hands.''

''I do. A little, I mean. With school and practice and homework—''

''How'd you like to talk about football three, four times a week?''

Bobby's eyes widened until they were almost as large as Mrs. Weeks'. ''Oh, man! Are you serious?''

Scott nodded. ''I need a stock boy. Part-time.''

''A job?''

''A job.''

''Wow. I'd have to make sure the hours wouldn't interfere with practice. Coach says—''

''I know what Coach says. What do you say tomorrow you give me your schedule, and we'll work around it. When we have our soda, that is.''

Bobby nodded vigorously. "Sure thing, Scott." He said the name as if it were underlined.

It was Scott's turn to thrust out his hand. The boy took it eagerly and, after a rousing shake, he let go and headed out of the bread aisle.

Scott wasn't quite sure how to feel about this little conversation. He was glad to have the help at the store, but he wasn't very comfortable with all that sir stuff. And he didn't want to talk about football. Not much, anyway.

He didn't want to be one of those guys who sat in bars and talked about the glory days. Not at twenty-six.

He looked at his watch. Another hour until he could get out of here. Meet with Emily. That would be good. Of all the people he knew in Sheridan, Emily and Coach were the two he respected most. Coach, because he was the best strategist in high school football. And Emily? Emily because, well she was Emily.

As he walked to the stockroom, he wondered if she was married. Probably. Smart men snatched up women like her.

EMILY SAW THE CHIP in her nail polish just as Scott walked up to the table. She smiled as if her manicure was perfect. He slid into the booth with a sigh.

"Hey, Em," he said so casually anyone would

think they met like this every week. In fact, she'd figured out exactly when they'd last sat down to talk. Senior year, graduation. Just before the ceremony was about to begin, Scott had walked right up to her, taken her hand, and led her to a bench on the quad. Her heart had pounded so furiously she was sure he could hear it.

But his stealing her away wasn't quite as romantic as her imagination presumed. He thanked her for all the times she'd listened to him go on about school and Cathy and football. He thanked her, in his shy, stumbling way, for helping him with English. And then he said goodbye, even though it wasn't even summer yet. He'd said goodbye like he wasn't ever coming back.

Who would have guessed that nine years later they'd be sitting in the last empty booth at Zeke's Place? That the afternoon sun would stream through the holes in the plastic window shades in such a way. That he'd look at her with the same friendly eyes. As she thought it, she realized with a start that his eyes weren't the same at all. They were older, although not by much, but that wasn't the thing. Her memory of that day in the quad was vibrant inside her, and the most vivid of the memories was the look of excitement in Scott's eyes. A look that held every promise, a look a man might have just before a great voyage. Now, his eyes seemed dull, defeated. She hoped it wasn't so. "You look tired."

"I am." He signaled the waiter, who came right to the table. "I'll have a Corona." He looked at Emily.

"Iced tea, please."

The waiter nodded and left to get their drinks. Then it was just her, Scott and the butterflies in her stomach. Tired or not, he still did it for her. Did it in a major way. A small part of her wanted to tell him how she'd loved him back in high school. But then sanity reared its blessed head. "So," she said, steering the conversation in the direction it was supposed to go, "why are you so tired?"

He shook his head and her gaze was caught by his hair. The overhead light showed his subtle highlights, but it was the thickness that made her want to touch it. "The store. It's taking a lot more work than I imagined."

"I was so sorry to hear about your father."

"Thanks. I miss him."

"I'll bet," she said, amazed that even though he still made her nervous, it wasn't all that hard to talk to him. In fact, it was more like old times than she ever would have imagined. "And I'll bet your mother misses him, too."

"Oh, yeah. She's having a hard time of it."

"How wonderful that you could come back to help."

His jaw flexed, and his gaze shifted away. He put down his menu, then moved his water glass an inch to the left.

"Rather be somewhere else, eh?"

His eyes widened in surprise. "How did you...?"

"You may be a great football player, Scott, but you're as subtle as a bull moose."

He grinned. "Boy, some things never change."

"Pardon?"

"You never did have a problem telling the truth, did you?"

She shrugged. "Only to myself."

He studied her for a long while, as if he'd just realized who she was. What was he seeing? Was he marching down memory lane, too?

The drinks came, distracting him.

"Want to talk about it?" she asked.

"What?"

"Where you'd rather be?"

The left side of his mouth quirked up. "This is just like high school, remember?"

"The library."

"And the bench by the fountain."

She remembered each and every time they'd talked like this. In fact, her diaries, long relegated to the back of her closet, held almost verbatim transcripts of their discussions. Every word had been golden to her, and she'd thought him the funniest, sweetest, smartest guy in the world.

At least that had changed. Oh, he was funny and sweet and smart, he just wasn't a deity anymore. But he sure was gorgeous. All sorts of muscles in her body contracted at that thought. She knew he was human, that he had faults, that he more than likely wasn't the least bit suitable for her, but she didn't care. She still wanted her night. One night where she'd catch him staring, unadulterated lust shining in his eyes. Was it too much to ask for?

"Those were good times," he said. "I'm not sure if I ever really thanked you for your help with Cathy."

Pop. Her bubble burst at the mention of Cathy Turner. The belle of Sheridan High, and the one person in the whole world that Emily hated. Not that she knew Cathy all that well, but every time she'd run into her over the years, Emily had been left with a bad taste in her mouth.

Cathy had been the head cheerleader, and that about said it all. Perfect little body. Perfect hair. Perfect clothes. And most annoying, a perfect boyfriend.

She waved away the thanks. "I want to hear what's going on now."

"I'm glad to be helping Mom out with the store, but…"

"But?"

"But the timing sucks."

"Why?"

"I was supposed to go for an interview tomorrow. At ESPN. The sports network."

She nodded. "An interview for what?"

He leaned in, his eyes lighting with a hint of that old inner fire. "It's a brand-new idea. Something no one's tried before. They're going to send someone to all the high school teams to profile the best players, the stars of the future. And they want someone young to do it."

"You'd be good at that."

He nodded unselfconsciously. "I would. That's the thing. I'd be perfect for the job, except—"

"Except you're back here, and ESPN is in Connecticut."

"How'd you know that?"

She smiled enigmatically. "I know everything, Scott. Don't you remember?"

He laughed at the old joke, but his heart wasn't in it.

"Your mother, does she know?"

"Oh, no. She doesn't have a clue."

"And I suppose you're not going to tell her?"

"I don't want her to feel worse than she already does."

"What are you going to do?"

His answer was delayed by the arrival of their

waiter, finally ready to take their orders. Scott wanted a burger with all the trimmings. So did Emily, but she ordered a salad instead, dressing on the side, of course.

"I'm going to work at the store," Scott said as soon as the waiter left: "Mom won't sell it. I've already asked about that."

"And no one else can run it for her?"

"She doesn't trust anyone but me."

"I understand."

He shook his head. "I don't know if I do. I mean, why would this plum of a job fall in my lap, just to be snatched away like this? It doesn't seem right."

"It isn't right or wrong, Scott. It's not personal at all, even if it feels like it is."

"Believe me, I've tried being stoic, and it works for a while. But then the reality of what I'm missing comes up and whacks me in the face."

"I'm sorry."

"Thanks." He sat for a moment, lost in the thought of a future that wasn't to be his, then took a big swig from his beer. "What's your story?" he asked.

"Me? No story. I teach. I enjoy it. I'm still tight with The Girlfriends."

"Oh, man. I haven't thought of that in years. You guys were crazy."

"We still are."

"Good. Some things shouldn't change."

Emily watched as he leaned back in his chair and looked around the diner. There were lots of places to eat in Sheridan, but when someone asked if you wanted a cup of coffee what they really meant was if you wanted to meet them at Zeke's Place. The service was good, the decor inoffensive if bland, and the coffee strong and pure, none of that latte half-caff for Zeke.

Emily had been coming here since she was a girl, and she'd sat in this very booth and whined about the man across from her. How he didn't know she was alive. How he kept going out with that horrible Cathy Turner.

She'd loved him for so long, it was as much a part of her as her hair, her eyes. Why couldn't she get over him? It would make life so much easier.

"You have a husband?" Scott asked.

She shook her head.

He shrugged and her gaze went to his broad shoulders, but she couldn't think about those now. "I figured you'd be married by now. Have a kid or two."

"Me?"

"Sure."

"I don't even have a boyfriend. I mean right now. I have had a boyfriend before, don't get me wrong, but he moved to San Antonio. So no, I don't have a..." She shut her mouth before she made things worse. *Change the subject, Em.* "What about you? You must have a wife."

He shook his head. "No."

"Girlfriend?"

"Not really."

"What does that mean?"

"I was seeing someone, but it wasn't serious. She wouldn't like it here anyway. She's a city gal."

"Ah. No Cathy Turner, eh?"

"That ended after high school."

The food arrived before she could shout "Yippee," saving her from utter humiliation. Her salad seemed as interesting as a brown paper bag, while Scott's burger looked amazingly delicious. She poured on a little dressing, and dug in with all the enthusiasm she could muster.

He didn't have a girlfriend! Of course, she'd known Cathy Turner was history. Cathy had married and divorced. She and Scott had been apart for ages, and yet there was a small part of her that couldn't help putting the two of them together.

"I never thought I'd be back here," he said. "Not to live, I mean. I worked so damn hard to get out."

"You don't like Sheridan?"

"You do?"

She nodded. "It's a wonderful town."

''It's in the sticks. There's nothing here. Nothing.''

She took another bite of salad as the roller coaster that was her life shot downhill. He hated it here. Once he figured out what to do about the store, he'd be gone. And she couldn't blame him. ESPN was an exciting job opportunity, and if that didn't come through, there would be something else. Something glamorous, someplace exciting. The high school teacher from Sheridan would disappear from his consciousness once more, as if she'd never been there at all.

''What's wrong?'' he asked, his burger halfway to his mouth.

''Salad,'' she said, wrinkling her nose. ''I'm not a big fan.''

''Want some of my burger?''

''No, thanks. I'd better eat my vegetables.''

They ate in silence for a few minutes and Scott devoured his burger. What an appetite! He'd always eaten a lot, more than anyone she'd ever met, and yet he had a six-pack stomach and the best butt in five counties. Another two bites, and the burger was gone. She hadn't put a dent in her salad.

''When did the Red Rock close?'' he asked.

''About two years ago,'' she said, remembering the old theater that had been such a part of her teenage years. "It just couldn't compete with the Cineplex."

He shook his head. "Too bad. It was a great place."

"Things change. It's inevitable."

"Not all things," he said with a smile.

"What do you mean?"

"You're the same. The same Emily I remember. Your hair, your laugh. You haven't changed a bit."

"I don't think that's a compliment," she said, her voice cool as a cucumber despite the fact she was screaming inside. The same *hair?* Oh God, he was right. She did have the same hair. And the same clothes, and the same dumpy body.

But not for long. Scott or no Scott, she was about to become the brand-new Emily Proctor.

Chapter Four

The next day Scott watched Cathy Turner walk out of his office. It wasn't an option, as far as he could tell. The way she sashayed was an invitation straight to her bedroom, reminding him of that old childhood saw, 'It must be jelly 'cause jam don't shake like that.'

He leaned back in his office chair, glad for the break, and glad that Cathy had come by. The years had been good to her, she seemed happy. The way she talked about her divorce made him think it was a good move for her. Prettier now than in school. She'd softened her hair and her makeup, at least that was his guess. He wasn't so terrific in the observation department. More than one of his girl-friends had complained bitterly when they'd changed their hair or bought a new dress and he hadn't noticed. He couldn't help it. He just didn't see things like that.

He'd better go back to the floor. Since he'd

taken over, business had been booming. At first he'd thought it was because everyone was glad to see the old place well stocked and cared for. But that wasn't it. Sure, the old customers came by, but the bulk of the new customers were from Pinehurst, which didn't make a whole lot of sense. Pinehurst had two Randall's, including a flagship store, an Albertson's and several specialty stores. Dillon's was known for its great produce, but still, it was too far to come for a good apple.

He wasn't complaining, though. His mother had felt good enough to come to the store in the afternoons at least three times a week, and it made her happy to see the parking lot full of cars, the aisles bustling with shoppers. She'd told him they were coming to see him, but that couldn't be true. Yeah, he'd been a pro football player, but that was then. This was now, and his new title was grocery store manager.

His thoughts returned to Cathy. Asking her out felt right. He'd always liked Cathy, even though she was an incredible snob. She laughed at his jokes, and she never ran out of things to say. She was easy to be with, and right now he didn't need any complications.

He collected his inventory book and headed out of his quiet office into the bustle of the store. After he spoke to Miguel, his produce manager, about next week's specials, he found himself thinking not of Cathy, but of Emily.

He'd had a good time yesterday. He'd felt more relaxed than he had in months. He wasn't sure what it was about her that made her so easy to talk to, but he was glad for it.

It had been a long time since he'd felt safe enough with anyone to really say what was on his mind. In the pros, he didn't dare hint that anything was less than perfect in his life. After, trying to land a job, was even worse.

But Emily...he should have kept in touch with her. She'd been there for him in high school like no one else. In fact, she'd helped him decide to go to Texas A&M, even though he'd wanted to go to Notre Dame. It had turned out to be the right choice.

It was great that she was still hanging out with her crazy friends. The Girlfriends had been no secret. The whole school had known about them and their pact to get together once a year no matter what. But that was the public version of the truth. In fact, it went much deeper than that. The Girlfriends had made a solemn vow to come to each other's aid in times of trouble. Not when it was convenient, or when they had time, but immediately, without question, period. Emily had told him they had each started a Girlfriends bank account using funds from baby-sitting so that if anything ever happened…

Emily had told him all this one night after he'd given her a couple of beers. It was senior year, and they were at Paul's house. His folks had gone to Branson for the weekend, and they'd trashed the place. Mostly, the football team. Not him and Emily. He'd never been one for partying like that. And Em? He'd found out afterward that she'd never had an alcoholic drink before.

But he'd thought at the time that Em wanted him to know about her commitment to her friends. The beer was an excuse. What he hadn't thought about was why. Why did she want him to know?

Oh, man, maybe it was her way of telling him she wanted to continue being friends, even after he went off to college. Yeah, that sounded like her. When Emily loved, she did it with all her heart. Unwavering, uncritical. He'd watched her over the years, all the way from fourth grade to graduation. She was slow to make friends, but when she did, it was for keeps.

He'd never really thought about that before. She was incredibly loyal, and she'd helped him see that it was important to stick with his friends no matter what kind of hare-brained things they did. According to Emily, that's when friendship was needed most.

He should have called her. He should have kept

in touch with her the way he kept up with Donny, his college roommate. They still talked a couple of times a month. And Gordon, they'd been rookies together, and they were still close. He'd worked at those friendships, mostly due to Emily's influence. The only important relationship he'd let drop was the one with her.

"You gonna stand there and stare at the toilet paper all day?"

Scott jumped, startled at the voice at his elbow. Sara Wilding, who'd worked for Dillon's for almost thirty years, gave him a look that told him he had about two seconds to take care of her problem. Sara was a force to be reckoned with, and he figured it was better to hop to it than test his supervisory clout.

"I need cash," she said. "Now." She handed him her voucher, then headed back to her station.

"Absolutely, Sara. And did I mention how beautiful you looked today?"

She grunted, not missing a step. Although Sara wasn't going to win Ms. Congeniality anytime soon, she was a good friend to his mother, and one hell of an employee. The woman never took a day off. She'd worked rain or shine four days a week since before Scott was born.

He headed back to his office and the safe. On his way there, he wondered about the group of teenage boys standing around the magazine rack.

They stopped talking the minute he walked by. He'd have to keep an eye on them.

He went to the wall safe behind his desk and twirled the combination lock. His thoughts weren't on the money inside, however. Instead, he had a rather startling realization. He wished his date for tonight was with Emily, not Cathy.

"CUT IT OFF. All of it." Emily closed her eyes as she waited for Denise to put scissors to hair.

"Are you *sure?*"

Emily opened her eyes again. "Yes, I'm sure. I want it short. I want it sophisticated, but mostly, I want it different."

"But don't you want to look at some more pictures?"

Emily's gaze moved from her reflection to Denise's. "I trust you. You're a wonderful stylist. So style."

"All right. Here we go."

Emily closed her eyes again as she heard the first snip. She hoped she was doing the right thing. She could end up looking horrible. No, Denise wouldn't do that to her. But it was going to be a very major change.

She no longer had brown, mousy hair. After a long, arduous morning of looking at color books and holding swatches to her cheek, she was a redhead. A deep, dark, rich redhead with soft golden highlights. And in a little while, that red hair was going to be short and interesting, and not at all *Emily*. Not the old Emily, at least.

She kept thinking about what Scott had said at lunch yesterday. It chilled her to the bone. She remembered, clear as a bell, the day they'd gotten their senior yearbooks. She and Zoey had found a nice quiet bench and were flipping the pages, joking about what silly things people write. Em's least favorite was "Stay just the way you are!" Who would want to be a geeky seventeen forever?

But that's just what she'd done, wasn't it? Stayed the same. Stayed safe. Built a wall of familiarity around her, and a wall of fat, too. She was well insulated from the world, and she'd gotten the life she deserved.

This was it. As more hair fell and Denise cut and hummed a Tina Turner song, she knew she'd taken more than a symbolic leap off the edge of a cliff. She was fully prepared to put aside her old ideas. To be open-minded. Willing to try new things. Adventurous.

Of course, there weren't a lot of adventures to be had in Sheridan. Except one. The greatest adventure of all: Risking her heart. It didn't matter how things turned out. It mattered that she ventured. That she tried. She wasn't going to look back at her life and have nothing but regrets.

Denise moved in front of her, blocking her view

of the mirror. She opened her eyes and got a glimpse of the mound of hair on her lap.

Oh, God.

It was too late to stop Denise. She'd finished the major cutting and now she was trimming. Em forced herself not to look. She wanted to see her hair when it was done, not before. She should have put on makeup, dang it. She always looked better with mascara and blush.

Her heart tapped wildly in her chest as Denise continued in her meticulous way. The humming got louder with each progressive snip, but all of Denise's clients had accepted that little eccentricity long ago.

"Almost there," Denise said.

Emily didn't let herself become excited. There was still the blow-drying to go. The hard part was not peeking. She had to think of something else.

Scott. Of course. Her favorite daydream. How incredible it was to have him here, in the flesh. She'd never really believed she'd see him again, which was, she supposed, why he was so safe to dream about.

He wasn't safe anymore, that's for sure. Being with him yesterday had stirred up all the old feelings and then some. The fact that he was here helping his mother when he could have been off chasing his own dreams said everything about him. He was a good person, a good man. His celebrity status hadn't swelled his ego disproportionately, his bad luck hadn't embittered him. He was still the same sweet Scott she'd fallen in love with all those years ago, only better.

The blow-dryer stopped. "You can open your eyes now," Denise said.

After a quick prayer to the hair gods, Emily did just that. What she saw made her gasp.

"Is it fabulous, or is it fabulous?" Denise asked.

"Oh, my." Emily said, although it was still hard to believe it was really her in the mirror. Why in hell hadn't she done this before? The red made her complexion fairly glow. Made her eyes look almost gold. But it was the cut that had taken her breath. Short and spiky, it flattered her face, making her cheekbones look higher and her cheeks thinner. She had to admit it, she looked good.

"You're stunning!" Denise said. Then she turned to the station next to hers. "Kelly, come here. You gotta see this."

Kelly, a relatively new addition to The Hair Port, took one look at Em and screeched so loudly Evelyn Todd peeked out from under her hair dryer. "You look incredible!" Kelly said, waving her scissors in the air, nearly cutting off the ear of her client, who had the good sense to duck.

"Em, you're a vision," Denise said. "Even if I do say so myself."

"It's...perfect. Better than I ever imagined."

Denise looked at her watch. "Do you have another half hour?"

"I have all day."

"Great. Stay there." She pulled her purse out of the cabinet drawer and hurried away, leaving Emily to wonder what was going on. In the meantime, she stared at her reflection, trying to get used to liking what she saw.

If only she didn't have a double chin. It wasn't huge, but it was there, reminding her that there was more to a transformation than a new hairdo.

She hadn't planned on going to the gym today, but she would. She'd work out on the machines so her hair wouldn't get too messy. And she'd ask one of the trainers what she could do about the chin situation.

"I'm back," Denise said, tossing her purse into the drawer. "And I've got makeup."

"Makeup?"

She nodded. "I've got some tricks up my sleeve. You'll be gorgeous." With that, she spun the chair around, pulled up a tray, then opened a black bag and took out more makeup than Emily had ever seen outside a department store.

"OH, MY *GOD!* You look like a movie star! Scott is going to fall at your feet and beg you to be his."

Emily smiled. "You're right, Julia. He's going to swoon."

"Don't be so darn cynical. You're gorgeous. Just admit it."

"I do like the new look," she said.

"I can't believe how brave you were. But look how it's paid off!"

"I'll be curious to see if I can duplicate it. The hair and the makeup. She made it look simple but—"

"Emily?"

She looked up at Donna Fargo, the waitress at Little Italy.

"It is you! Wow. What an improvement!"

Emily laughed when Donna realized what she'd said.

"I didn't mean…you've always been pretty. Oh, man." Donna hung her head. "Can we start over?"

"Sure," Emily said. "How about we start with a glass of wine?"

"It's on the house."

"You don't have to do that."

"Yes, I do. Merlot?"

Emily and Julia both nodded.

"I'll be back."

Julia smiled as she watched Donna retreat. Emily wondered how the woman was doing. Her husband had left her only four months ago.

"You want to share the spaghetti mari—oh, my God."

"What?" Emily put down her menu. Julia's eyes had grown wide. Really wide.

"Nothing."

"Julia!"

"Just don't turn around."

Emily turned.

"I said don't—"

But it was too late. She saw them as Donna was clearing their table. Scott and Cathy Turner. It was just like the old days, only Cathy dressed better now. Tonight, she wore a red blazer, tight blue jeans and a white shell, and she looked like a million bucks.

How had she missed seeing them? Had they been here when she arrived?

Emily deflated like a balloon. Suddenly her hair wasn't so smashing and the makeup was too much. She turned back to Julia. "So I guess I'm not the only old buddy Scott wants to catch up with." She picked up her menu, mostly to hide behind. "I don't want to share the spaghetti marinara," she said. "I want lasagna. And lots of it."

"No. You're not going to blow it. You think that stuck-up witch will have a chance against you?"

"She's already won, in case you haven't noticed."

"Bull. He's only out with her because she asked."

"How do you know that?"

"I don't. But I'll bet it's true. Besides, he took you to lunch first, right?"

"Don't panic, Julia. I'm not going to get the lasagna. And I'm going to be good tomorrow, too."

"Good."

"I'm not really doing it for him, you know."

Julia smiled. She was so effortlessly beautiful Emily could have been terribly jealous. But Julia was too nice to hate. "I wondered when that would happen," she said.

"You little sneak."

"Hey. It doesn't mean you won't get him."

"I won't. But it's okay. Honest. It was a crazy wish. I mean, I'm not the one-night-stand type." She shook her head. "It was a dream. A nice dream. And it served its purpose. It got me off my big old butt."

"Don't give up hope yet, my dear. Stranger things have happened."

"Like what?"

"Like Paul agreeing to come to dancing lessons with me."

Emily blinked. "Paul? Your Paul?"

Julia nodded. "It's a birthday present. We're going to take ten line-dancing lessons over the next five weeks."

"I don't believe it. He hates country music, and he hates dancing."

"I know." She grinned. "But he loves me."

Emily knew that was true. Paul Simpson was Julia's best friend. Even better than The Girlfriends. Paul and Julia had been joined at the hip since seventh grade, and they'd seen each other through good times and bad, good dates and bad. Emily had never figured out why they didn't take their friendship to the next level. Julia had told her once that she didn't want to risk the friendship, but Emily wasn't so sure that was it. Julia didn't want to risk her heart.

Which was something Emily understood all too well.

"Shh," Julia said, apropos of nothing. "They're coming this way.

Emily winced, then pasted on a bright, shiny smile.

"Hey, look who's here!" Scott brought Cathy to the table. "Julia, good to see you. You too, Em—" He stopped short. His brow creased as he stared at her. "You got your hair cut."

She nodded.

Cathy smiled. "It looks really good."

"Thanks."

"It does look good," Scott said. "It looks great."

Em felt her cheeks heat. "I'm pleased with it."

Her blush got hotter as she watched Cathy put her arm around Scott's waist. There was no mistaking the meaning of the move. Cathy had declared Scott as her own, planted her flag so to speak. Emily thought of telling her she needn't worry. There was no competition. Cathy was perfect. Her hair, her makeup, her figure, her clothes. It was no contest.

"I'll call you tomorrow," Scott said. "If you'll be around."

"Sure." Her gaze shifted from Scott to Cathy, who didn't look pleased. In fact, she looked ticked off.

"I'd like that," Emily said, feeling a guilty pleasure at rubbing Cathy's nose in it. "We can go catch a movie or something."

Scott nodded. "That would be great. And I really like your hair."

"Thanks."

"See ya."

Emily waved as Cathy practically dragged Scott out of the restaurant.

"You've got her," Julia said. "And she knows it."

"I do not." Emily shifted her gaze to the entrées, but her thoughts weren't on veal scallopini. She had a feeling that somehow, some way, Julia was right. She could have him. And Cathy knew it.

"I'm having a goat cheese and prosciutto pizza," Julia said.

"I'm going to have a salad. With dressing on the side."

"You go, girl. I gotta say, he is one fine-looking example of the male species."

"He is."

"And her boobs are fake."

"Julia!"

"They are. Fake, fake, fake."

Emily picked up her water glass. "To real boobs."

Julia tipped Emily's glass with her own. "Amen, sister."

Chapter Five

"Did you see that?" Lily said excitedly. "I can't believe it!"

Emily nodded although her face heated with a blush at her lie. She hadn't seen the last play, or much of anything at the game. She knew the Sheridan Tigers were stomping on the Waco Wolverines, but she had no idea what all the hollering was about.

"What's wrong?"

"Nothing," she said.

Lily's gaze went to the seats on the field. Right to where Scott was sitting with Cathy Turner, his arm around her shoulder. "Oh."

"It's no big deal." Emily leaned in front of Lily so she could see JT. "How's school going, kiddo?"

JT, in the manner of all eight-year-old boys, shrugged. "It's okay."

"Just okay?"

He nodded.

"How'd you do on that math test?"

"Okay."

Lily shook her head. "He got a ninety-four."

"That's wonderful!" Emily said, but then the capacity crowd roared as Sheridan made a field goal.

"Quit changing the subject," Lily said, after the din had quieted.

"I can't change a subject I was never on."

"Oh, please. This is so much like high school I can't stand it. The only thing missing is your braces."

"Cut it out, Lily. I'm not worried about it. Honest. So just keep watching the game."

Lily unzipped her purple fanny pack and took out her lipstick. Without the aid of a mirror, she applied the makeup perfectly, then she fluffed her curly hair.

"What are you doing?" Em asked, her radar telling her Lily was up to no good.

"Nothing. I'm just going to the bathroom."

"You are not."

"Excuse me? Are you trying to tell me you know more about my bladder than I do?"

"Yes. I do. You're not going to the bathroom, you're going to accidentally run into Scott and Cathy. You're going to bring up my name, and tell Scott where we're sitting. You're going to say something incredibly nice about me, and then give Cathy the hate stare.''

''And your point is?''

Emily sighed. ''Don't forget to mention my hair.''

Lily burst out laughing.

''And while you're down there, get me a hot dog.''

''No way. If you're hungry, eat your carrots.''

Emily stuck her tongue out at Lily, who smiled, got up and edged her way down the row.

Emily turned her attention to the game. Well, not really. She acted as if her attention was on the game. She leaned forward and peered down at the field. But she had no idea who had the ball, nor did she care. Football wasn't her thing. Never had been. In high school, she'd come to watch Scott. Then, when he'd gotten into college sports, she'd watched him on TV, always pleased when he did well, but not for the same reasons as the rest of Sheridan.

In this town, you didn't admit to being indifferent about football. The Sheridan Tigers were the most important thing in Sheridan, and the good townspeople went absolutely bonkers during the season.

Even now, so early in September, there was talk of city championships. Several people, who had perfectly respectable jobs and families, had actually painted their faces green and white in a somewhat twisted display of town spirit. If anyone knew she didn't know a touchdown from a down comforter, she'd be run out of town on a rail.

"Aunt Emily?"

She turned to JT. "Yeah?"

"Do you really know Scott Dillon?"

She nodded. "Sure."

"Think you could ask him for his autograph?"

"Really? You want his autograph?"

JT nodded. "Oh, yeah. That'd be great."

"Your mother knows him, too," she said.

"She does not."

Emily smiled. "Wanna bet?"

JT's eyes widened. God, but he was a beautiful boy. Blond hair, shining in the afternoon sun, blue eyes, a smile that could light up the sky. She loved him completely. She'd been there for his birth, and she'd been there that first hard year, when Lily had been so sick. JT had become the child of The Girlfriends, and it was caring for him that had sealed their friendships and their sacred pact. "Your mother went to school with him, just like me."

"Are you sure?"

"I'm sure." She scanned the risers and spotted Lily just as she approached Scott. "Look," she said, pointing so JT could see for himself.

JT followed her finger, and when he saw the

evidence for himself he got so excited he shot up out of his seat. "She never told me!"

"Did you ask her?"

He shook his head, his eyes practically popping out of the sockets. "I can't believe it. Wait'll I tell Jake. And Sean. They're gonna croak."

Lily must have told Scott where they were sitting, for he turned to scan the seats. Emily jerked back and grabbed JT by the shirt, forcing him to sit down.

"Hey!"

"Watch the game."

"But he's looking up here."

"I know. That's why we can't look back."

"But—"

"JT, if you don't look at Scott for the next ten minutes, I'll get you his autograph and his old yearbook picture."

"Wow."

"Wow, indeed," she said, forcing herself to watch the play while every nerve in her body screamed to know what Lily was doing. But for the next ten minutes she hardly moved, hardly even breathed. She was the picture of rapt attention, a fan of the team, of the game. JT mimicked her posture in his determination to win the prize.

The sounds around her shifted suddenly from indistinct chatter to a low murmur. It could only mean one thing. She turned to find Scott in the aisle, standing with Lily, but without Cathy.

"Hey, Em," he said.

"Hi."

Next to her, she heard JT's gasp. Evidently, Scott heard it too. "You're JT, right?" he asked.

The boy managed a nod.

"Real nice to meet you. I understand you're something of a football fan."

Again, all JT could do was nod. The look of adoration on his face made Emily like Scott more than ever.

"I can't stay long, but I wanted to say hi." Scott turned his attention to Emily. "I was wondering if you'd be interested in coming down to the locker room with me after the game."

"Me?" she asked.

"All of you. Just for a few minutes. There's kind of an open house thing coach does once a season. Letting parents and friends into the inner sanctum. So I thought, if you weren't busy—"

"Yes!" JT shouted.

Scott grinned.

"I guess we'll take you up on that offer."

"Great. Meet me at the entrance to the gym, okay?"

She nodded. He waved at JT, said something to Lily that she couldn't hear, then dashed down the stairs. Her gaze went to his seat. To Cathy, who was looking right at her. Their eyes met over the hundreds of people in the stands, and even at this distance Emily could feel Cathy's animosity. Emily turned to JT, much preferring his unbridled enthusiasm. The boy was so excited he couldn't sit still, and when Lily rejoined them, he gave her a hug that nearly choked her.

"See," she said to him. "I do have my uses."

"I'll say!"

Emily laughed, but her thoughts were on her imminent encounter with Scott and Cathy. Her stomach clenched in a way that was too familiar.

It was just like high school. Emily had always been the third wheel. Never the main attraction. She'd been in too many situations where she had to smile and act as if everything was perfect when she was dying of envy inside. Aching to be the one who could touch Scott's chest, or take his hand. It wasn't just Scott and Cathy, either. It was all the couples from the freshmen to the seniors, pairs of lovesick teenagers exploring each other like newly discovered countries.

She'd watched them. She'd never been one of them.

In college, things had gotten better, but not by much. She'd met Jerry, and after a long, awkward courtship they'd become a couple. Sweet Jerry with his fumbling hands, his inept kisses. He was a nice guy and Emily had tried to love him.

The crowd around her leaped to their feet, screaming bloody murder, but Emily didn't join in. She hardly heard the roar. If it wasn't for JT, she'd go home right this second. Just leave. She didn't want to be anywhere near Cathy. It was too painful to watch her touch Scott.

"What's wrong?" Lily asked. "I thought you'd be happy."

"I am. I'm delighted."

"You don't look delighted."

"That's just in contrast to the maniacs next to me."

Lily frowned, clearly not buying her story. "Come on. Let's go. I don't want JT to miss any of the players."

"The game is over?" Emily asked.

Two people from the seats just below her turned to her with scandalized expressions. She laughed, as if she'd just been making a big joke.

"You are too much," Lily said. "With all the football games you've been to, you still don't get it, do you?"

"Nope. I'm convinced it's genetic. I wasn't born with the football gene."

"Come on," JT said, desperation making his voice unnaturally high.

Emily followed the crowd down the stairs, then waited for Lily and JT, who'd been stuck behind a slow-moving older man, to join her. Together the three of them headed toward the gym.

Each step brought more anxiety, more dread. She didn't like it. Didn't like the part of her that lived in jealousy. She had a wonderful life. A job she loved, the dearest friends in the world. It shouldn't matter one whit that she didn't have a boyfriend. That she didn't have Scott. But it did. It mattered something fierce.

She wanted, just once in her life, to look into a man's eyes and see love there. Love for her. She wanted to hear the words, and to believe them. She wanted to be cherished, to be adored.

She wanted the fairy tale.

It was safer to focus on JT as he bounced across the field, literally jumping for joy. He was such a great kid. Lily had done a wonderful job raising him by herself. Emily wondered briefly if Lily would ever marry. If she'd ever find a father for her son.

The real father was a mystery, even now. Although The Girlfriends shared their lives with each other, there was still the question of who JT's biological father was. When she'd gotten pregnant, they'd asked her time and time again. But the questions stopped when it became clear Lily wasn't going to tell. No one cared much anymore. They were all just grateful to have JT.

Emily rarely thought about having a child of her

own. Not because she didn't want one but because she wanted one so desperately. It was all supposed to have been easier than this. She should have found love by now, with someone real, someone she could build a comfortable life with. She knew Scott wasn't the man for her. He was destined for a big life, when she would be most content with staying here in Sheridan. Teaching. Having a couple of kids.

They reached the locker room and JT bounded inside. Lily followed, and after a moment of hesitation when she toyed with the idea of running for cover, Emily walked in, too.

It was chaos inside. Players, family, local news reporters, fans all chattered loudly, celebrating the victory over the Wolverines. But Emily barely noticed anything but the man standing next to the Coach. She wondered if Scott realized he'd mimicked Coach's posture with his arms folded across his chest, his legs spread wide. The two of them were a study. Coach, a colleague of hers now, who had helped form the lives of so many young men. Who'd taught responsibility, dedication, persistence. Whose greatest victories weren't on the playing fields, but in the hearts and minds of his boys.

"Listen up," Coach bellowed. "McFarlane, knock it off. Potter, put that down. Listen up," he repeated as the last of the miscreants stopped roughhousing. "Because this is family day, we're going to do things a little differently. We're gonna have our pictures taken and some of us are going to be interviewed by the Sheridan High Gazette. But first we need to do a little business." He cleared his throat, then took a step to his right, leaving Scott as the center of attention. "Scott here has something he wants to say."

Scott nodded at Coach, then took two steps forward. "I liked a lot of what I saw out there. The defense was tight, passing was good, and you worked like a team."

At that, the boys clapped and hooted raucously. Scott let them have their shout, but then he held up a hand and the room grew quiet again.

"There were also some things I didn't like." He walked over to the blackboard on the side of the room, forcing the team members to huddle close. Emily and Lily stayed where they were, leaning against the far wall. JT looked up at Lily with pleading eyes and she nodded. He darted past lockers and around benches until he was right in the center of the huddle.

That's when Emily realized Cathy wasn't there. Nudging Lily, Emily whispered, "Where is she?"

"She's not here," Lily whispered back.

"Where did she go?"

"How should I know?"

"But—" Emily's voice caught in her throat as

the team turned to stare at her. She smiled, then put a finger up to her lips to indicate she'd be quiet now.

Scott started in again. ''Left tackle was offside four times. You need to do a better job of remembering the count. Also, the quarterback and wide receivers need to communicate better. On defense you need to blitz more. You're giving the quarterback too much time in the pocket.''

She didn't understand some of what he said, but that was okay. She saw what effect he had on the boys.

They sat rapt, listening with all their concentration. There wasn't a sound in the place, other than Scott's low, even voice. Once again she was reminded that he wasn't the boy she knew. He was a compelling man who wore his fame like an old sweater. He really did deserve a big life. He would be extraordinary on television. Women would love him and men would admire him. Just like they did now.

Scott talked to the team for about twenty minutes, and in that time she watched him earn a legion of fans, if they weren't that already. He also earned her respect in a totally new way. He should teach. Coach. Of course, being a sports commentator was much more glamorous, and God knows it paid better, but it was a shame. He had a gift.

That gift would make him an ideal father. He

didn't belittle even as he criticized. Instead, he empowered the boys to go farther, run faster, try harder.

Lily leaned over. "He's wonderful. Look at JT."

Emily slid her gaze to the boy who was now in the front row, and in his eyes she saw dreams being built, untold glories waiting in the wings, a whole universe of possibilities.

Coach stepped in and took over. Scott spotted Emily and headed her way, but first he stopped by JT and put his hand on the boy's shoulder. JT fairly quivered with the thrill of it. The two of them came over to the lockers. Scott seemed exhilarated from his pep talk.

"So, what did you think?" he asked.

"You're good with them," Emily said. "I'm a bit envious."

He shook his head. "Nah, don't be. I'm just imitating the master. Coach is the one who deserves the credit."

"Sorry," she said. "I'm afraid not. You might have learned from him, but I was watching you."

He smiled, and if she wasn't mistaken, she'd swear his cheeks turned pink.

"I've got to get going," Lily said as she deftly took JT's hand. "This one has homework."

"Aw, Mom!"

"Don't 'Aw, Mom' me. You promised you'd do

your homework tonight if I let you come to the game.''

"But—" He looked from her to Scott and back again.

"Maybe we can do this again next week," Scott said. "And maybe, if it's all right with your mom, you guys can come sit with me."

JT's face lit up like a Christmas tree. "Can we?"

Lily nodded. "If you do your—"

But the last word was drowned out in a holler that shot up through the rafters.

"Excuse me while I take Tarzan home," she said. "Scott, can you give Em a ride home?"

Emily had been totally unprepared for that. What was Lily thinking?

"Sure. No problem."

"Okay then." Lily took off for the door, which was the only thing that saved her life. "Bye!"

Then she was gone, and Emily was left alone with Scott. And the team, of course, but they might as well have been chairs for all the attention she paid them.

"So it's just you and me."

"What happened to your date?"

His smile faded. Or maybe it didn't. It might have been a trick of the light. "She had to go. Her folks are coming in from New York and she had to pick them up at the airport."

"That's too bad."

He didn't say anything. He put his hand in his pocket, turned to Coach, then back to her. "You busy later tonight?"

She almost said yes. She didn't want him to know that she had absolutely nothing planned on a Saturday night except laundry. But she'd never lied easily. "Nope."

"How about having dinner with me?"

"Are you sure you don't want to wait for Cathy to come back?"

"No. I don't. I'd really like to have dinner with you, Em."

"I suppose we can work something out."

He smiled at her. And she fairly quivered with the thrill of it.

Chapter Six

Scott put his menu down and looked around the restaurant. He hadn't been to the Pump Room in years, but nothing about it had changed. The same dark carpet, wood veneer walls. The small lamps at each table, and especially the big leather chairs that had impressed him so as a child. But his gaze didn't linger on his surroundings. Instead, they went to the woman across from him.

"It's the strangest thing," Scott said. "Half the boys on the football team have applied for jobs at the store."

Emily smiled. "And you can't figure it out?"

"No. I mean, we don't pay slave wages, but we're also not handing out big bucks."

"Scott, they aren't coming for the work. They're coming because you're there."

"No."

"Yes."

He thought about that for a moment. Could she

be right? Could the boys be there because they respected him? Or was it just that they considered him a celebrity of sorts? He drank his coffee, then looked once more to Emily. "Do I need to do something about this?"

"I think you're already doing it."

"What?"

"You're listening to them. Talking to them as if they matter. You care about what they care about."

"That's it?"

"Of course."

"How do you know this stuff?"

"Because I'm a teacher. Because I know a little something about high school boys. But mostly because I've heard you talk to them."

"I don't get it. I mean, there's a whole subculture of groupies that hang around the pro football teams. But I never figured it would be like that in my own hometown."

"I don't think they're groupies. Not in the same sense."

"Then what?"

She looked down for a moment, then met his gaze. Her eyes were soft and kind. A deep brown, with bits of gold. "I think they're coming to you because of what you can teach them. You've done it. You've reached a cultural Mecca. You've been a pro football player, and that's the top of the world to these young men.''

"I can't make it happen for anyone. It doesn't work that way."

"No? Didn't Coach help you?"

He nodded. "Sure. He encouraged me. He made sure I learned discipline and perseverance."

"That's what you get to pass on. You can help teach these boys about all those qualities. They probably won't make it to the pro leagues, but the skills will help them in whatever field they choose."

"Teach them, huh?"

She smiled. "You've certainly got what it takes."

"I never wanted to be a teacher. It wasn't even on my backup list."

"But you're good. And I think it's good for you. I watched you in that locker room. You're a natural."

He sat quietly, thinking about her words. Comfortable with the silence between them.

"They're looking for a father figure," she said. "Between you and Coach, they're very lucky."

"Father figure? Me?"

She laughed, and the sound made him smile. "Yes, you. You'll make a wonderful father when the time comes. Trust me."

He wasn't ready for that bit of information. Not yet. He might still get that job at ESPN. Or another one like it. He focused on Em, pushing the issue of fatherhood far into the recesses of his mind. She looked pretty with her hair like that. Had she always been this attractive and he hadn't noticed?

"What's wrong?"

He shook his head. "Nothing. I was just thinking about how pretty you look."

He was rewarded with a bright blush. "I'm not," she said.

"Of course you are. I'm never wrong about these things."

"You're not, eh?"

"Nope."

She took a deep breath, and in that moment he saw a swirl of emotions in her face. Surprise, embarrassment and finally a grudging acceptance. "Thank you."

"You're welcome," he said, thinking about how different she was from Cathy. Cathy took compliments as her due. She knew she was beautiful, and she expected others to acknowledge thc fact. But he had the feeling Emily had no idea she was pretty.

The waiter came to the table and handed them both a list of the restaurant's famous pies. Scott didn't need to look. "French apple for me."

"I'm not much of a pie person," Emily said, handing the menu back to the waiter.

"You sure?" Scott asked. "They're really good here."

She shook her head. "No, thanks. But I will have another cup of coffee."

Scott handed his own menu to the waiter. Just as he was turning back to Emily, he saw Jim Heeps, the wide receiver for the Tigers, at the table behind them. In fact, there were five members of the football team, and all of them were looking at him.

He nodded, then turned back to Emily. "We've got company."

"I see."

"I don't get it, but I guess you're right."

"I'm never wrong about these things."

He grinned. Then something shifted. He couldn't explain what. He certainly didn't understand it. But it was as real as the tablecloth. Emily changed. Right before his eyes. She suddenly wasn't Emily from English class anymore. She'd grown into a woman. A fine woman. "I thought about you," he said, surprised at his own confession.

She froze for a second, her cup halfway to her mouth. "You did?"

"Yeah. I did. I thought about our talks. You were really something, you know that? And now I see you still are."

"Stop it," she said, her cheeks turning pink

again. She was so flustered she nearly spilled her coffee when she put the cup back on the saucer. "You're embarrassing me."

"I'm not trying to. I'm just telling you the truth. It was always you and Coach. You two got me through all the really important things in high school. If it wasn't for you, I think I would have gone crazy with all those recruiters. Jeez, remember that guy from Virginia?"

She nodded. "He was such a jerk."

"A jerk with a really big expense account."

"But you didn't succumb."

"Mostly because of you." He smiled as another memory swam to the surface. "You used to hit me all the time."

"I did not!"

He nodded. "Yeah, you did. You hit me on the shoulder. Not maliciously or anything, but you'd just kind of slug me whenever you were trying to make a point."

She opened her mouth to protest, then closed it again. "It was a habit I broke, thankfully."

"I'll say. It hurt."

"No."

"Yeah. It did. You had a real powerhouse punch there."

"Me?"

He nodded.

"I would have stopped if you'd said something."

"I couldn't. I was the captain of the football team."

"Ah, I see. Male pride."

"It's not something to laugh about. Especially in high school. Wasn't it you who taught me about the influence of hormones on life decisions?"

She laughed. "I was so full of it."

"No you weren't. You were bright as hell. You meant a lot to me."

Her gaze went to the water glass, to her fork, to the window. Then finally she looked at him again. "What about... No, never mind." She shook her head.

"What about what?"

"Well, what about Cathy?"

It wasn't what he thought she was going to say. He had to shift gears quickly. "I don't know," he said, deciding right that second to be completely honest. "She's a great girl, don't get me wrong. But not for the kind of things I'm talking about."

"What kind of things was she great for?"

The waiter came to the table with his pie and the coffeepot. A few moments later, after a bite of French apple, Scott considered Emily's question. "She was good for me socially," he said finally. "Before Cathy, I'd always felt terribly uncomfort-

able at parties and things like that. I never knew
what to say.''

''And after you met her?''

''She's great at small talk. She'd always have
something to discuss, some new diet or exercise
program. Or she'd talk about the kids at school.''

''That interested you?''

''Sometimes. But other times, it just meant that
I wouldn't have to say much.''

''So you must be glad to see her again.''

''I am. But it's no big thing. I'm not going to
be here long enough for anything to happen.''

''Does she know that?''

''Oh, yeah. I told her.''

Em nodded slowly. ''I see.''

''What?''

''You might have told her, but she didn't believe
you.''

''What do you mean?''

''She wants some of your magic, too. But not
the same magic.''

He ate pie for a while and listened to the sounds
around him, watching as a young couple who were
obviously in love sipped champagne. The Pump
Room was the nicest restaurant in town, and he'd
only been there four or five times. On his prom
night. After graduation. But back then, he'd been
uncomfortable here. Now he realized it was a nice
restaurant by Sheridan standards, but it wasn't in

the same league as Le Cirque or Spago. "I needed Cathy," he said. "I can't explain it, but she gave me courage. Not on the field, but at parties and at places like this. She always made it seem easy."

"I'm glad you had each other," Emily said. But her voice had changed. Hardened. The way she played with her cup told him something was wrong.

"Em?"

"Hmm?"

"I—" He stopped suddenly as the boys from the team came up to their table.

"Hey, Scott," Jim said.

"Hello, guys. What can I do for you?"

"We just wanted to say thanks. You know, for the bull session and all. It was great."

"My pleasure."

"We were just talking about that Hail Mary you made at the All Star game. That was so fu—" He looked at Emily, then shuffled a bit to his right. "That was so great."

"Thanks."

"What was your favorite play, Ms. Proctor?"

In a little dance that was becoming familiar to Scott, Emily grabbed her cup as her face heated pink. "I liked them all," she said.

"Yeah, but you gotta have a favorite," Jim said. "Right?"

She shook her head. "I couldn't pick. There were too many wonderful moments."

Jim opened his mouth to say more, but Bobby Knight poked him in the side with his elbow.

"We just wanted to say, like, uh, thanks," Bobby said.

"Sure thing, boys."

Tom Whittaker, the tackle, waved, then the whole gang hurried out of the restaurant, careful not to bump into any chairs or tables. Scott was reminded of bulls in a china shop. He turned his attention back to Emily. "No favorite plays, eh?"

"Not one in particular."

He tried hard not to grin. "Do you know what a Hail Mary is?"

She opened her mouth, then closed it again. "No."

"You're not into football, are you?"

She shook her head. "But I think *you're* terrific."

He laughed. "Boy, if I didn't have an ego the size of Texas, my feelings would be hurt."

"Hey. I like you as a person. Not a football player."

His laughter stopped immediately. Of course. That's why he'd liked her so much. Why he'd asked her here tonight. Why he looked for her when he went into town. "Well, I like you right back."

Her pretty little blush told him he'd said the right thing.

He finished his pie, content just to be at the same table as Emily. Boy, if things had been different...

She sure did look nice with that red hair.

THE PHONE WAS RINGING when she walked into her apartment. She flung her purse on the kitchen counter and plucked the receiver from the cradle. "Hi, Lily."

"How'd you know it was me?"

"How many times did you call?"

"Only twice."

"Liar."

"Okay, so I called seven times. The point is, what happened?"

"Nothing happened. It was a nice dinner, that's all."

Lily sighed. "What about Cathy?"

"She wasn't there. It was just Scott and my-self."

"And nothing happened?"

"That's right. We ate. We had some coffee. We talked."

"Talked about what?"

Emily opened the fridge and stared at the pitiful contents. Water, celery, fruit, yogurt, chicken breasts. Not one piece of pie to be found. "We talked about him, mostly."

"Duh. He's a guy, isn't he?"

"But we also talked about me. About teaching and stuff."

"Did he ask you about your love life?"

"No."

"Bummer."

"It's late, Lily. I need to go to bed."

"Okay. But first tell me what you ate."

"Why? I stuck to the diet."

"I don't care about that. Well, yes I do, but not right now. I just want to hear what it's like to go to a fancy restaurant."

"You've been in fancy restaurants, Lily."

"Not for ages and ages. What did you have?"

"A salad and a piece of grilled tuna."

"I bet there was parsley on the plate, right? Maybe a thin slice of lemon?"

"Both."

She sighed again. "Come over tomorrow."

"I have papers to grade. My lesson plan."

"Do it early and come over. We'll watch *Pride and Prejudice*."

"I'll call you."

"Night."

Emily hung up the phone then headed for her bedroom. She did want to go to bed, but not quite yet. She wanted to think about dinner. About one particular moment at dinner. Not when he said she was pretty, although that was incredible all by itself, but the moment before the football players came to the table. When he'd looked at her. When he'd started to tell her...what? What would he have said if he hadn't been interrupted?

There was no way to ask him. None at all, and she'd thought about it all the way home. The only thing she could do was hope he'd try again.

She looked in the mirror as she took off her earrings. She'd lost weight. She could see it in her cheeks, and most especially her double chin—or lack thereof. It wasn't totally gone, but it was getting there.

She turned sideways, lifting her shirt so she could see her stomach. Flatter. It was definitely flatter, although there was still a pooch. She hadn't weighed herself for almost two weeks. Mostly because she knew if she hadn't lost weight she'd probably give up. But tonight she had a feeling she'd feel good about the number on the scale.

After she finished undressing, she went to the bathroom. It was a little chilly, but that was only because she was naked. She stepped on the scale. 151! She'd lost nine and a quarter pounds! Unbelievable!

She stepped off the scale, waited a moment, then climbed back on. Same result. Same incredible result!

The diet was working, and for the first time in years Emily felt truly hopeful. Not that her whole life was centered on her weight, but it was far more important to her than she liked to admit.

This time, she was going to do it. She was going to get to her ideal weight, and she was going to stay there. First thing in the morning, she was signing up for weight training at the gym. And spinning. Because she wanted more than a thin body. She wanted a fit body.

Man, what a night. First, Scott told her she was pretty, then this. Maybe he *had* been trying to say that he wanted to change their relationship, that he wanted to date.

The way he'd looked at her...

She shivered, then grabbed her nightgown from the back of the bathroom door. She needed to do some serious shopping. All her underwear and her nightgowns were old and ugly. Utilitarian. Boring. She was almost ready to go to phase two of her makeover. But not yet. She wanted to take off at least ten more pounds.

Except for that horrible moment when she'd admitted she didn't care for football, the dinner had been a smashing success. She'd never admit this to any of The Girlfriends, but she'd been a little worried about spending any real time with Scott. What if he'd become a jerk? What if all the things she liked about him weren't really parts of him, but her own imagination?

But she liked him. She liked him a lot. Despite

what he'd said, he didn't have a large ego. In fact, he listened in the most thoughtful way. Most men, in her experience, listened to hear confirmations of their own beliefs. Not Scott.

In fact, when she talked to Scott she felt as if her words carried a great deal of weight with him. She felt important.

She got her toothbrush from the cup and attacked her teeth with gusto. Every night for what felt like her whole life, she'd brushed at least twice a day, for two minutes each time. But tonight she didn't care about the state of her plaque. There were more important things to think about. So she finished up, rinsed and put the brush back in under a minute.

It was liberating. Sheer defiance. The new Emily might get really wacky and, gasp!, go to bed without taking off her makeup! Oh, no! The world would probably come to an end. At the very least, the media would have a field day: Emily Proctor Changes Habits. News at 11:00.

She grinned at herself. God, she had cheekbones. Real cheekbones. It was unbelievable.

She turned to head to bed, but just as her hand touched the light switch, she paused. This was no time to break out. Not when things were spicing up with Scott. Why tempt fate?

The light remained on as Emily went back to the sink. First cold cream, then tissue, then a nice wash and rinse, then moisturizer, then eye cream, and while she was at it, a quick rub of her elbows followed by more moisturizer on her hands and arms.

There. That was better. She could go to bed. Perchance to dream. And she knew just what she wanted to dream about.

She flipped off the light, then crawled under her comforter. She'd dream about him in his football uniform. With those wide shoulders and that tight little end of his. Sighing, she turned over to hug her pillow. It wasn't as if she had a butt fetish or anything, but Scott's butt was quite extraordinary. That wasn't opinion, but fact. Every girl at Sheridan High had known that.

Maybe, if the gods continued to smile down on her, she'd get to touch that hiney one day. And his chest. Oh, man, his chest. It was perfect.

He was perfect.

Ten more pounds, and she'd be…no. She'd never be perfect. But she'd be pretty darn good. She closed her eyes and sighed, then she sent up a small prayer of thanks. For the first time in ages, she was excited about life. Excited about the possibilities. She was doing something about her situation and she felt in control.

Maybe, if she stuck to her diet and did her exercise religiously, she wouldn't have to settle for one night with Scott. Maybe she could have a lifetime.

Chapter Seven

Scott hung up the phone, not sure at all why he'd turned down Cathy's invitation to lunch. He had time now that four more football players had signed on as part-timers. Each one of them was doing more than their share, and after his discussion with Emily, he understood that they were trying to impress him. Emily had been right about a number of things. He should have called her, but all week he kept thinking he'd run into her. Maybe he'd give her a call tonight.

He left his office, checking the time as he walked onto the floor. It wouldn't be long now. In an hour, he'd start interviewing the candidates for store manager. It was the right thing to do, he felt sure of that. He'd finally broken down and told his mother about ESPN. She insisted he find someone else to run the store. She didn't want him to miss out on the possibility of a great career in television.

Yet, he felt guilty. There was no mistaking the

clenched stomach, the quickening pulse, the furtive glances toward the door.

"Hey, Scott."

He jumped at the feminine voice, spinning around to see Hope Francis smiling up at him.

"Sorry. I didn't mean to scare you."

He waved her apology away. "It wasn't your fault. My head was somewhere else."

"I know how that can be."

"It's good to see you," he said. "What are you doing in this neck of the woods?"

"I was across the street, Gina's Fabric. I'm going to actually try one of those home craft projects Samantha is always so hot about."

He nodded. "Samantha. She was the one who made all her own clothes, right?"

"That's her. Now she's got me convinced that I can make my own duvet. I figure if I screw it up, I'll just buy one, and tell her I made it."

"Good plan."

"Thanks."

He smiled, expecting her to start shopping, but she didn't move. "Is there something you need?"

"Oh, I was just wondering if you'd seen Emily lately."

"Not since last week."

"Really?"

He nodded, not quite understanding her tone. It

was a mixture of surprise and, if he wasn't mistaken, anger.

"Too busy with Cathy, huh?"

Whoa. This was getting strange in a hurry. "Nope. Too busy with the store."

"I see," she said, but her right brow raised ominously.

"Am I missing something? Was it her birthday?"

"It wasn't her birthday, but you are missing something."

"What?"

"If you don't know, I can't tell you."

He looked over the diminutive woman before him, exasperation making him want to wring her little neck. He remembered when she had long hair, and how she used to twirl a strand around her finger all the time. She'd been his lab partner in chemistry one year, and he'd thought about asking her out. But Cathy would have had a fit. "What does that mean?"

She raised the other brow. "A smart guy like you should be able to figure it out."

"I have no idea what you're talking about."

She sniffed. "That figures."

"Hope, you're making me nuts."

"Oh, for heaven's sake. You can't even see what's in front of your nose. I swear, you men."

She shook her head, then headed off toward the

produce section, leaving him mystified. What was that all about? Maybe Hope thought he was someone else. Or maybe she was having a psychotic episode or something. Very weird.

But The Girlfriends had always been a mystery to him. Except for Emily, of course. Emily. He really should call her. But first, he had to see to some interviews.

WHOEVER'D INVENTED the StairMaster should be shot. And Emily was just the gal to get the job done.

Her thigh muscles screamed in protest, and if she panted any harder she'd probably burst a lung. Two more minutes. She could do this for two minutes. She just had to think of something other than her poor legs.

Scott. Why hadn't he called? It had been a week, and every day that the phone didn't ring, she'd grown more disillusioned. It was too much like high school for her taste. Back then, she'd been positive he liked her. Even though she hadn't been very popular. Or pretty. But their talks had been so wonderful, so meaningful, that she'd believed with all her heart that Scott would wake up one day to realize he loved her, not Cathy.

It never happened. And it wasn't going to happen now. He hadn't called, and even if he did, she knew it wouldn't be for anything more than a nice chat.

Oh, why was she making herself so crazy? With a minute left to go, she switched off the horrid machine. On shaky legs, she turned to go to the locker room. Only, someone called her name. She looked over at the treadmills, but her smile died on her lips when she saw Cathy Turner in her tiny, perfect leotard and tights, her hair up in a disarmingly perfect mess, her skin fairly glowing.

"Hi, Cathy."

"I didn't know you came to this gym," Cathy said, her breath perfectly even and strong.

"I just joined a week ago."

Cathy eyed her, taking in the bulge of her stomach, the way her thighs rubbed together. "They say they can work miracles here."

"Is that so?" Emily knew she'd just been dissed, but she wasn't about to let Cathy have the satisfaction of seeing her react.

"I was just telling Scott last night that there was this huge woman in my aerobics class who's lost nearly forty pounds."

"Good for her." Emily smiled, calling on her latent acting skills. "I've got to dash. See you around."

Cathy nodded imperiously as Emily headed toward the locker room. She knew beyond a shadow of a doubt that Cathy was looking at her rear end, shaking her head at how fat it was. But Emily wouldn't walk faster. She wouldn't.

Once she rounded the corner, she stopped and leaned against the wall. She wiped her face and slowed her breathing, trying not to get crazy. It didn't matter what Cathy Turner said. It didn't matter how rude she was, or what her agenda had been. Emily wasn't huge. And even if she was, so what? People like Cathy made her ashamed of giving a moment's thought to weight.

After another deep breath, she continued her walk, and once she was inside the locker room, she made a point of going to the mirror. No, she didn't have an ideal body. Not by a long shot. Her thighs, her stomach, her butt were too big. Not nearly firm enough. And so what?

Was that what she wanted, to judge herself by the standards of the Cathys of the world? To derive her sense of worth from her dress size?

She sighed, slumping against the lockers behind her. That's exactly what she wanted. She could lie to herself that she just wanted to be healthy, but deep inside she knew that she'd always felt less worthy, compared to the skinny girls. None of her good qualities had ever made up for being fat.

She looked into the mirror once more, trying to see herself as she really was. A teacher. A friend. A daughter. A woman of passion with a love of words. But none of the sobriquets told the awful truth of her inner thoughts. She was a fat girl. She'd always been a fat girl.

She didn't have to stay a fat girl. But she'd better be damn clear why she was losing the weight. Was it for herself? Or was it for Scott? If he left, would she stop dieting? Stop exercising? Did she have enough respect for herself to take care of her body, for no other reason than that she deserved it?

A woman she didn't know passed her, giving her a critical glance. Emily felt the urge to hide, to dash behind her locker door. For whom? For what?

She'd better figure this out, and soon. And she'd better figure out just why she wanted Scott Dillon so fiercely. Was it love? Or did she, like all the others, just want some of his magic?

SCOTT KNOCKED AGAIN, louder this time. She might not be home. Or she might not want to see him. Or…jeez, he didn't know what was going on. Hope's bewildering visit hadn't let him be all day. He'd called Emily twice, both times hearing her cheery message to leave his name and number. Then he'd tried to do some bookkeeping. But he'd had to do the bank reconciliation four times, so he figured it might be wiser just to get himself over to Emily's and find out what was what.

Her apartment had been simple to find. In this

little town, all he'd had to do was open the phone book.

It was a nice place. A little old, but it had character. There was even a swimming pool in the complex, which was unusual for Sheridan.

With a quick glance at his watch, which told him he'd been on her front stoop for over five minutes, he debated again if he should knock or leave. Knocking won, and this time he banged on the door, more out of frustration than because he thought she couldn't hear.

"No matter how hard I've tried to teach him, my cat still can't open the door without a little help from me."

Scott whirled around to see Emily. Her smile made him feel better immediately. "I wasn't sure if you were home."

"I wasn't," she said. She put down her canvas bag and stuck her key into the lock. She stepped inside and turned to face him. "But I am now."

He grinned. "You busy?"

"Nope. Except that my doorknob-challenged cat needs food, and I need to change clothes."

"Why?"

She laughed. He was glad he came by. She sure didn't look angry with him. What had Hope meant?

"I've just been at the gym, and I'm all icky."

"Funny, you don't look icky."

"Football players have no concept of icky." She led him into an airy living room. Right off the bat, he saw it suited her. It wasn't an ordinary room at all. The couch was old and overstuffed, but he couldn't quite tell what color it was because she'd draped afghans over it. Bright pillows fell on top of one another in a friendly heap.

A collage of pictures decorated the mantelpiece, the walls were painted a warm peach, and then there were the books. Tons of them, lining two walls. Hardcovers, paperbacks, big old picture books. She used all manner of things as bookends. The closer he got to the shelves, the more he saw her fingerprints. There was a plastic hula boy doll, the kind people put in the back of their cars. And a fishbowl with fake fish. The big sculpted apple, bright red and shiny, was undoubtedly her nod to her profession, but the bust of Mozart said more about her than anything else. Not because she was so into classical music, but because Mozart was wearing X-ray specs, the kind he'd seen in the back of comic books alongside Bazooka Joe jackets and Magic-8-Balls.

"Can you make yourself comfy while I shower?"

He nodded. "Sure."

"There might be a beer in the fridge. I know there's root beer."

"Thanks." He spotted a miniature chess set, but the pieces were characters from *Star Trek*.

"Scott?"

He turned to face her, even though he hadn't gotten to half the shelves. "Yeah?"

"Did you come here for something special?"

He shook his head. "No. I just hadn't seen you around. If you have something else to do tonight, I can be out of here in two seconds flat."

"No. Please stay. I'll be back quick as a wink."

He noddcd, but she didn't see him. She'd already headed down the hallway. His gaze traveled down her body, and he wished she wasn't wearing such a big shirt. He couldn't see any curves at all, when logic told him there should be some very impressive curves. But she'd always liked those baggy clothes, even in high school. He remembered one sweater. It had been all different colors—bright blues and reds and purples. She wore that thing all through tenth grade. Different jeans, different turtlenecks, same sweater at least once a week all through the fall and winter. He could pick her out of any crowd.

Turning back to the books, he saw a stack of magazines on the bottom row. *Sports Illustrated.* That didn't make sense. The woman didn't know what a Hail Mary pass was. He crouched and picked up the top issue. He recognized it. He'd been interviewed by Bob Costas. The magazine under that also had an interview. Every one of the magazines had something about him in it.

He wasn't sure how he felt. More pleased than anything. Curious, too. Was it just because he was a local boy who had done well? Or because they'd known each other in school? Or had she bought these magazines because...

Because why? He stood up, his gaze latching on a row of Stephen King paperbacks. Emily was his friend. Of course she'd keep magazines like that. He'd keep magazines if she'd been interviewed. Wouldn't he? Yeah, sure. Of course.

A meow from behind lent the perfect excuse to forgo this train of thought. He turned to see an enormous cat, at least twenty-five pounds and none of it fat. Yellow and white, with yellow eyes, the cat was a real beauty.

The cat rubbed his chin on the edge of the bookshelf, then meowed again. The voice wasn't right. It was too high, too shaky. The cat version of Katherine Hepburn. But he looked friendly enough. Scott crouched once more. The cat walked boldly up to him and Scott scratched him in the important places: behind the ears and under the chin. He had a fan, if the purring was any indication.

"What do you think?" he asked the cat. "Did I do something stupid?"

The response was a long raggedy meow, which Scott couldn't interpret. So he got up and went to the kitchen. Emily's white refrigerator door was a gold mine of eclectic doodads. Make your own poetry tiles, some of which were in a jumble on the upper right-hand corner, and a few choice words she'd put together. *Fingers trace the edge of her lips.* Under that, *Longing with a quiet sigh.*

Next to the poetry stood *David.* Michelangelo's *David.* Only hers wore surf trunks and a Hawaiian shirt. A picture of The Girlfriends had a place of honor in the center of the fridge. He liked it. They were all laughing, and he could see it was genuine, not for the camera. There was Zoey with her wild hair, and Sam, whom he'd wanted to know better. Enigmatic Hope, Lily, with her secrets, and Julia, picture perfect even when no one was looking. In the center was Emily. Her smile as warm as sunshine, her eyes the kindest he'd ever seen.

"Didn't you find anything to drink?"

He opened the door quickly, not wanting her to know he'd been staring at her things. At her. "Just looking. You want something?"

"A root beer, please."

He grabbed a can for her, and a beer bottle for him. "Didn't you used to drink this in school?" he asked, turning to hand her the soda.

She wore a long green dress. It had some flowers on the pockets. Her hair was still a bit damp but incredibly shiny, and she smelled great.

"I did. I'm something of a root beer junky, if

you must know.'' She popped the top of her soda and sat down at the kitchen table. He joined her, admiring the teak salt and pepper shakers. Next to them was a bowl of fruit. Fresh fruit that looked good enough to have come from Dillon's. ''So what really brings you to my neck of the woods?''

''I hadn't seen you in too long.''

''You could have. I was right here.''

''I know. I got busy with the store. I think I've bitten off more than I can chew.''

''You could run that place with one hand tied behind your back.''

''It's not that. It's all my new employees. Five of them in all, each on different shifts, but none of them available during practice or school. They're trying real hard.''

''So what's the problem?''

''They all want to talk.''

''And you oblige?''

''Yep. Get me started and I just keep on going like the Energizer bunny.''

''I wouldn't worry too much. It sounds like things are working out just fine.''

He took a swig of beer, then stared at her poems again. *Longing with a quiet sigh.* He understood that. The job of his dreams was slipping out of his fingers, and there was nothing he could do about it. ''Tell me about your life,'' he said, turning back to Emily.

"You know my life."

"No, I don't. I know the big picture, but none of the details."

"Fair enough." She drank a little more soda and her brows creased in concentration. "This isn't so easy."

He nodded ruefully. "Tell me about it."

"Oh, yeah. I bet you've had to tell your life story lots of times."

"Don't change the subject."

"Yes, sir. Okay. I was born in a shack on the Tallahassee River—"

"The truth, please."

"Spoilsport."

"Start with your job."

She smiled. A good sign. "I like it. A lot. The kids, they're terrific. For the most part. And those who aren't present a particular challenge. But mostly, I like teaching drama."

"Oh, man. Juliet!"

"Romeo!"

"You were good. Way better than our production deserved."

"You weren't so bad."

He burst out laughing. So hard, in fact, that she had to join him. "I sucked."

"Yeah. You pretty much did."

"But they could hear me in the back row."

"Honey, they could hear you in Tunisia."

Bits and pieces of his past flew around in his head. Rehearsals, opening night, giving Em flowers. She'd cried. She'd cried for a long time. "Are you happy, Em?"

She quieted. Her smile faded. She looked him square in the eyes, unblinking. "For the most part, yes. I am."

"What would you like? To make it perfect, I mean?"

"Perfect? There's no such thing."

"But if there were?"

She shifted her gaze. Toyed with her can of soda. "Love," she said, so softly it was like her poem. "Love would be wonderful."

He leaned forward and slowly brought his fingers to her cheek. She closed her eyes. He traced her upper lip, then her lower lip and when he was finished, she sighed.

He wondered what it would be like to kiss her. Then he leaned across the table.

Chapter Eight

Emily held her breath, her heart beating so wildly she thought he must hear it. He must know that his touch had electrified her. That this was the moment she'd been waiting for. Longing for.

He leaned closer. She felt his warm breath on her lips, then closed her eyes once more. But the kiss didn't come. His breath disappeared and she opened her eyes to see him sitting back in the chair, his face a mask of bewilderment. *Oh, God.*

She jumped out of her chair and went to the kitchen sink, turning away from Scott. Her face burned with humiliation, the memory of her encounter with Cathy stinging all the more. She turned on the water and washed an already clean cup.

"Emily?"

She didn't turn around. She prayed that he'd leave. Just leave and never come back. It was all too horrible.

"Emily? I'm sorry. I don't know what I was…I had no business…"

"It's okay. Fine. But you know what? I forgot that I have a bunch of papers to grade. I'll be up half the night with them. So if you don't mind?"

She heard his chair scrape. "I'm sorry. I—"

"It's nothing," she said, far too sharply. She turned to face him, praying he couldn't see her shame. "But I really do have to get to those papers."

He nodded, but he didn't move. He looked at her with concern in his gaze. Regret. Embarrassment. She could hardly stand it. If he didn't leave right now, she'd burst into tears, which would make things impossibly worse. It was too hard. She just couldn't face him. "You can find your way out, right?"

"Yeah. But I hate to leave it like this."

"Like what? I'll talk to you later. Maybe we can do lunch or something."

"Okay," he said, but he didn't sound convinced. It hardly mattered. It got him to move, to get out of the kitchen. To leave the scene of the crime.

She slumped into her chair as soon as she heard the front door open. When it closed, the tears came. Hot, burning tears that streaked her chubby cheeks.

The moment, the hideous moment when he'd

backed away, replayed over and over in her mind. The moment he'd realized he was with *her*. With Emily Proctor. The girl with the braces and the size-fourteen dresses. The girl he came to for advice. The girl he never asked for a date.

Why had she told her friends she wanted Scott? If she'd only kept her mouth shut, this could have been a private hell. What were dreams for anyway, if you couldn't ever hope to have them come true?

She felt Boo rub against her leg, his soft fur comforting in its familiarity. He meowed, letting her know that despite her world crumbling around her shoulders, he still needed to be fed. She forced herself to her feet. Got the cat food out of the cupboard. It calmed her a bit, actually. At least she had Boo. He loved her, and he didn't give a damn about her thighs.

He attacked his food with a gusto she completely understood. It made her wish she had more than celery sticks and chicken breasts in the fridge. She could always go out. Maybe drive through the Taco— No. No. She wasn't going to eat over this. She wouldn't give that to him. Or Cathy. They weren't going to take this away from her, too.

She'd show them. She'd show them both. She was going to lose all the weight she needed to, and she was going to get so buff Jane Fonda would ask her for tips. Determination swelled inside her, pushing the humiliation out of the way. She could do this. She *would* do this. Scott or no Scott, she was going to be the best Emily should could be.

She got up, went into the living room and turned on her stereo. She looked through her CD collection until she found an old Chaka Khan. Pushing the volume up three notches, she pressed play, and when the music started she closed her eyes. She moved her head, her hips. When Chaka wailed her heart out, Emily danced. She danced with abandon, with fury. She danced until she could hardly catch her breath, not caring the least what she looked like. No one could see her here. No one could flinch away, or give her a cruel once-over.

The heck with the neighbors. She danced until she ached. Until she had to stop, her legs shaky and tingling. It took her a long time to catch her breath, but by the time she did, she felt better. The hell with Scott Dillon. She'd never really loved him. She'd had a schoolgirl crush on a cute boy. Well, from this day forward Scott was going to be the last thing she thought about. She'd embarked on a new journey. She was going to discover who Emily was, and who she could be.

No more tears. No regrets. Just the future, as bright and shiny as a copper penny.

Boo meowed his approval.

SCOTT WENT BACK TO THE DOOR for the fourth time. The music was playing so loud he didn't even bother to knock. She wouldn't have heard him.

He headed toward his car, beating himself up with every step. What had he been thinking? He'd blown it with the one person he could really count on. The one person who liked him for who he was, who was his friend. Emily was too important to him to screw it up just because she smelled so sweet. Because her cheeks were so soft and her eyes so warm. He had no right to touch her at all.

But then, what was that business with Hope? She'd been talking about Emily, he felt sure, but what was the message? Was he supposed to back off? Or was it—?

"Oh, damn," he said, climbing into his GTO. Maybe he wasn't supposed to back off at all. Maybe...?

No. He would have known if Emily was interested in him that way. He'd never had any trouble deciphering such things, and he knew Emily better than most people. He'd have sensed it. She'd have given him a signal.

He didn't start the car up immediately. He just sat there, staring at Emily's apartment building, wishing he knew what to do. Things had been so simple only a few months ago. Before his injury. He'd loved playing football. He'd loved every minute of it. The games, the workouts, the other guys, the planes, the press, the fans. His days had been determined by the schedule, and even on his time off, he'd always had something interesting to do.

But, he realized now, he hadn't had to make many choices. And no particular woman had caught his eye, so even there he wasn't faced with anything difficult.

That was the problem, of course. The situation had been the same in school, in college. He'd never had to make the kind of choices he was up against now. Even his decision to go to Texas A&M had been pretty straightforward. Cathy had been there in high school, and in college he'd dated casually. Pretty women. Nice women. But no one like Emily. No one who understood him like her.

So what was this about? He definitely wanted to kiss her. Hmm. Maybe because that was so new. He hadn't thought about her this way in high school. She'd been a friend, someone he'd opened up to. That wasn't the case any longer. Maybe it was her new haircut, but he doubted it. Mostly, he was attracted to her because of the way she made him feel.

But one thing he'd learned in the pros—don't mess with something that works. If it ain't broke, don't fix it. His relationship with Emily was the only relationship that wasn't broken. His mom— that one was complicated as hell. He wanted to do what was right, but it killed him not to grab on to the best opportunity a guy his age could ever expect. Cathy? She was turning into something of a problem, although he hadn't realized it until just now. Emily was right, he could see that Cathy wanted more. Cathy wanted him to be in love with her. But he wasn't. Which brought up yet another dilemma. Knowing his feelings, should he still go out with her? Have sex with her?

He banged his hand on the steering wheel, cursing fate, cursing his own limitations. The one person who could help him sort things out was upstairs, mad at him. Perfect.

It was getting late. His stomach grumbled and he realized he hadn't eaten since around eleven. It was seven-fifteen, and he didn't want to go home, or eat by himself. The only thing he could think to do was go to the Long Horn Saloon. They made good burgers, and they had lots of booze.

He'd never been one to drown his sorrows in liquor, but tonight it seemed like a hell of an idea.

"WHAT TIME IS IT?" Emily turned so she could see her alarm clock, the phone hurting her ear as she rolled.

"It's twelve-fifteen."

"In the morning?"

Hope sighed. "Yes, in the morning. You need to get up."

Emily's heart thudded in her chest. "Who died?"

"No one died. You just need to get up and go over to the Long Horn."

"What are you talking about?"

"It's Scott. He's drunk."

"He's a big boy. He'll find a way home."

"Em, Cathy is there. She's talking about flying to Vegas. To get married."

Emily was awake now. And the memory of this evening's debacle was right there to welcome her. "If that's what he wants to do, then there's nothing I can do about it."

Hope cleared her throat. "Pardon me?"

"You heard me. I don't care if they go to Vegas. I don't care if they go to Timbuktu."

"What happened?"

"Reality hit the fan."

"This is no time to get maudlin. You need to get up and go over there. Get him away from Cathy."

"Why?"

"Because you're his friend, that's why."

Emily stared at the lump under her covers that was her cat. Boo wouldn't let a simple thing like a drunken friend disturb *his* sleep. But then, Boo didn't have many friends. Emily did, and despite what had happened, Scott was still her friend.

"Emily?"

"Yeah."

"Are you going?"

"Yeah."

"Good. If you need help, call me."

Emily hung up the phone, but she didn't get right out of bed. She thought about the consequences of going to the saloon. Cathy wouldn't be pleased to see her. Scott probably wouldn't be, either. It would be messy. So why bother? Why get tangled up in their business?

It was no use. She wouldn't be able to go back to sleep now, so she might as well go. Maybe have a drink, play a little pool. If she happened to run into Scott—

Oh, who was she kidding?

She pushed aside the covers and headed for the bathroom. Her muscles hurt in her thighs and calves, but it was a good hurt. Unlike the pain in her heart. Who knows? Maybe saving Scott tonight would help her see him in a new light. As a friend, nothing more.

THE BAR HAD A BIG CROWD for such a late hour. Emily didn't recognize many people. There was Alan, the bartender. She nodded his way, and after he acknowledged her he turned toward the far side of the bar. She saw Scott, leaning on his elbows, a shot glass and a half-empty beer glass sitting in front of him. And Cathy. Hanging all over him.

Emily didn't move. She stared at the two of them, watched as Cathy laughed so loudly she could be heard all over the bar. Scott didn't even smile. He just stared at his drink. Cathy, unsatisfied, leaned over and kissed his cheek, nudged him in the side. Although Emily couldn't hear the words, she got the drift. Cathy wanted to go. Now. Before Scott sobered up.

Em took a deep breath, then headed into the fray. She knew it was going to be bad the minute Cathy caught sight of her. Cathy's brows came together menacingly, and her lips pursed in a scowl that made Emily's hair stand on end. This was not a woman who wanted to see her.

"Hi there, Cathy," Emily said, as lightly and innocently as she could manage. "Fancy running into you."

"What are you doing here?" Cathy asked, keeping her voice low, just above a whisper. Even so, Scott heard her. He turned his gaze toward Emily.

"I'm here for a drink. Same as you."

Alan approached with impeccable timing. "What'll you have, Em?"

"How about one of your famous martinis? With two olives."

He gave her a warm smile. "Coming right up." Then he turned to Cathy and his grin faded.

"I'll have another beer," she said. "And so will my friend."

Alan glanced at Emily again, and she gave him a subtle shake of the head. He smiled at Cathy, nice as you please. "Sorry, Cathy. But you two have reached your limit."

"You can't do that!"

"Yeah, I can. I just did. And I'm gonna call a taxi to come take you home."

"I don't need a taxi."

"Sure you do. You can come back and get your car tomorrow."

"But I'm not going home." She looked at Scott, shook his arm. "We're going to Las Vegas. Aren't we, honey? Scott?"

"I don't think so," Emily said. "Not tonight. Tomorrow, when he's sober, you can discuss it again."

Cathy's face filled with fury. "Butt out, Emily."

"I wish I could. But it doesn't look like I'm going to."

"This is none of your business."

"It is. Scott is my friend. And I'm not going to let him mess up his life by taking off to Vegas with you."

"You bitch!"

"Yep, that's me. Now, why don't you have a cup of coffee while we wait for the taxi?"

"You're amazing," Cathy said. "You think he'd look at you? You think he thinks of you as a woman? Wrong. Ha." Her voice had risen until she was practically shouting. "He thinks you're a cow. Everyone thinks you're a big, fat cow."

"Fine," Emily said, trying not to let the drunken words bother her. "I'm a cow. That doesn't change the fact that you're going home, and so is he."

"Try and make me."

"She doesn't have to," Alan said, coming around the bar. "Because I can make you. The law says I can. So either you come with me and wait for the taxi to take you home, or I call the police and you spend the night in jail."

"Do you know who I am?"

"Yes, ma'am," he said. "You're drunk. And you're eighty-sixed as of right now."

Cathy's mouth opened, but no words came out. Alan took her by the elbow, and after a brief tug-of-war, she went with him. As they passed Emily, Cathy gave her a positively lethal glare, but Emily was too amazed at the sight of Cathy's clothes to care. The woman was wearing a shirt so tight it would have been illegal in four states. Her pants were equally tight, leaving nothing to the imagination. Was that what appealed to Scott? Oh, God, no wonder he'd stopped before he kissed *her*. She'd never dream of wearing anything that tight. Not even if she had a perfect figure.

"Where's Alan?"

The slurred voice behind her brought her attention back to Scott. He looked like hell. For Scott, that is. How did some men stay handsome as sin, even when they were three sheets to the wind and sinking fast? Despite everything, as she slid up onto the bar stool next to his, her traitorous heart beat a little harder. A little faster. "Hey there, Cowboy."

"Emily."

"That's right. Emily."

"Oh, man, am I glad to see you."

"I'm surprised you can. Those eyes of yours are fairly swimming in booze."

He shook his head, a monumental effort it seemed. "How'd everything get so screwed up?" he asked.

"I wish I knew."

"I called my answer—" he hiccuped "—my answering machine. Guess who it was?"

"I don't know."

"Come on. Guess."

"Regis Philbin."

He gave her an odd look, then shook his head as if he wanted to make the jumble of letters in his head mean something. "My manager."

"Oh?"

"They didn't hire anyone yet."

"Oh."

"He said they still want to see me."

"What did you say?"

"I said I couldn't. My one chance to really be

somebody, and I have to stay in this stinkin' little town at that stinkin' little store.''

Now she understood the drinking. She'd never known Scott to have trouble with alcohol. Given the circumstances, she supposed she could forgive this trespass.

'''N' I called Coash. Coach.''

''About what?''

''A job. Coashing. Coaching.''

''At the high school?''

He nodded, then wiped his mouth with the back of his hand. ''There's no budget.''

''You want to coach?''

''There's no budget in any of the high schools. So I'm out of luck. And that's why I need another tequila.''

''No, you don't. What you need is to go home and get into bed.''

''Yeah. Bed. But first just a little more.'' He held up his hand, holding his finger and thumb an inch apart.

''I'll give you some,'' she said, ''at your place.''

''Okay.''

She slid down off the bar stool just as Alan returned. ''Is she in the cab?''

He nodded. ''How about the football star?''

''I'll take him home, Alan. Thanks.''

''He owes me some money.''

"I'll make sure he comes by tomorrow. Oh, and I guess I'll have that martini another time."

"No sweat. You be careful."

"I always am." With that, she put Scott's arm around her shoulder and helped him off his stool. They both teetered for a dangerous moment, then he seemed to find his feet. He listed heavily toward the right, but she figured she could get him into her car.

It took longer than she'd expected. He managed to spill half a pitcher of beer on himself and her, anger the nice fellows who had intended to drink said beer, and then *she* had to pay for a replacement pitcher. But the really tricky part had been getting the door open while he tried to escape back into the bar.

She finally got him into the car and buckled up. She took a moment to catch her breath, and to look at him. Drunk as a skunk, smelling like a brewery, leaning back on her headrest, eyes closed, six-o'clock shadow nearing midnight. And she still wanted him. What did that say about her sanity?

She quickly got behind the wheel, and headed for his mother's house. He didn't say a word. In fact, the only sound he made at all was a very indelicate snort.

But he came to with a vengeance as she pulled into his mother's driveway.

"I'm not going in," he said, his voice less

slurred, his eye more focused. "I want to go back to the bar."

"No."

"I'll get out here. Call a cab."

"No, you won't."

"Then take me back."

"Scott, settle down—"

He grabbed her arm. "I can't go in there. I can't face her like this. I've already caused her enough trouble."

The desperation in his voice might have just been the alcohol talking. Or this whole thing might be an exercise in guilt and sorrow. She'd give him the benefit of the doubt. "I won't make you go in. But I won't take you back to the bar."

He nodded. "Your place."

"Oh, no."

"Please, Em. I need you."

She closed her eyes for a moment, then gave him a critical glare. "That's the way it is between us, isn't it? *You* need *me*. Well, what about me? Don't I ever get to be the one in trouble? The one who gets to lean on your shoulders?"

"Aw, Em. I'm a lousy friend. Just plain lousy."

"No, you're not."

"I am."

"Fine. You are. Now sit back." She put the car in reverse and backed out of the driveway.

"Where are we goin'?"

"Where do you think?"

"Aw, Em," he said, his voice almost weepy with gratitude.

"Oh, just go to sleep, would you?"

Chapter Nine

It took some doing to get Scott to her apartment. When she finally shut the door behind them he stopped leaning on her and looked around as if he was surprised to find himself at her place. When his gaze moved to her, he grinned as if she hadn't been with him all this time.

"Em!"

"Hello, Scott."

"Em," he said with a sigh.

"Yes. I know. Now what do you say we put you to bed?"

His smile widened and he teetered to the right, then the left, then finally came to a stop in the center. "Emily. I knew it would be you. You come through like a...like a..."

"Chump?"

"A chump! That's it. No, wait."

She didn't. She left him standing in the living room and went to her linen closet. Pulling down a sheet, a blanket and a pillow, she remembered that she had a pair of men's pajamas in a box under the electric blanket. She'd meant to give them to her father for his birthday, but then she'd found the tennis racket he'd been searching for. So she still had the pj's. They'd be big on Scott, but so what? He couldn't sleep in what he had on. His shirt and jeans were still damp with beer. It took a minute to find the box of pajamas. When she did, she grabbed them and the linens and headed back to the living room.

He stood where she'd left him. Maybe swayed was a better word. Back, forth, and back again, he looked as if he were standing on a boat in rough seas. She shook her head, wondering what character flaw in her makeup kept landing her in situations like this.

Ever since seventh grade, when Hope and Julia told their parents they were spending the night with her when they had actually gone to a concert with two ninth-grade boys, Emily had been the rescuer. Maybe she should get one of those miniature wooden casks to put around her neck, like the Saint Bernards wore in the Alps. Although the last thing Scott needed right now was brandy.

She moved him five paces to his right, then proceeded to make the couch into a bed. When she turned back to him, she saw he hadn't budged. Oh, heavens. What a sorry sight.

She pulled him over to the couch and handed him the pajamas. "Put these on."

He looked at them as if he'd never seen pajamas before.

"You take off your clothes, and put these on. It's easy, really."

He opened his mouth. His brows creased. Then his mouth closed.

She sighed. Maybe she should just leave him in his smelly jeans. They'd dry eventually. He certainly didn't deserve nice clean pj's. And as for her washing his clothes tonight? No way! Not her. Not this gal. Filled with righteous indignation, she went straight to her room, slamming the door behind her.

EMILY CURSED HERSELF for a sap as she moved her fingers to the second button of Scott's shirt. She'd gotten back into her sleep shirt, brushed her teeth for the second time that night and crawled into bed with Boo. Only, the light in the living room hadn't gone out. Not after five minutes. Not after ten. She'd gotten up, but only because she didn't want to pay an enormous electric bill.

When she'd seen him sitting up half-asleep, his clothes on, the pajamas on his lap, she resigned herself to the fact that she was going to help him even though he didn't deserve it. Even though she shouldn't.

She reached the last of the buttons on the part of his shirt that wasn't tucked into his jeans. Yanking the rest of the shirt out woke him up a little. Not much, but a little.

"Hi," he said.

"Hi."

"What're you doin'?"

"Playing Parcheesi."

He smiled with half his mouth, which she figured was appropriate. It hadn't been that funny. Then he closed his eyes again.

She reached for the lower two buttons and the back of her hand brushed against his warm skin. A shiver hit her all the way to her toes. *Oh, God.* It would be terribly inappropriate to touch him again. She couldn't. Of course not.

She undid the last two buttons in a seriously businesslike fashion. Unfolded the pajama tops. Pulled the right sleeve of his shirt off, then the left. Grabbed the pj's.

And then her shoulders slumped. "Who am I kidding?" she whispered. Scott didn't move. He was already asleep. So what difference would it make if she touched him? If she let her hand slide down over the muscles and smooth skin? She wasn't harming anyone. It wasn't against the rules to touch.

The heat of him surprised her. But nothing else did. She'd imagined touching him a million times, pictured her fingers toying with the sparse dark hair on his chest, his hard little nipples, strumming his washboard stomach. The only thing was, in her dreams, he'd been awake. Awake, and returning touch for touch, caress for caress. He'd whispered naughty things in her ear while he explored her body inch by inch.

Her hand went to the top button of his fly, then retracted. Could she? No. It would be too personal. But then, it was his own fault for being drunk, right? Why not? She touched it again, the top button. It took her a few seconds to get it undone, mostly because she kept expecting him to jerk awake and ask her what she thought she was doing. But he didn't. His eyes stayed closed. God, his eyelashes were long. That didn't seem fair. She'd trade hers for his in a heartbeat. But that wasn't the subject at hand. She'd just undo the second button. That's all.

He had on white shorts. Boxers, which she preferred. They made her think of that scene in Bull Durham when Susan Sarandon burst in on Kevin Costner while he was ironing and—

Scott moaned. She jumped up, her face heating with guilt. She waited, not moving an inch. Not breathing. But he wasn't up. The moan hadn't been about her.

She should go to bed and forget about him.

Throw a blanket over his shoulders. He'd be fine. Besides, she was tired. It was terribly late.

Well, maybe she'd try one more time to get the job done. She sat down and before she could change her mind, she'd undone the last of his buttons. There. All she had to do was pull off his pants. Put on the pj's. Help him lie down. Simple. What any friend would do. Hmm. Maybe she'd start with the top.

It might have been simple, but it wasn't easy. His arms kept flopping down before she could get the sleeves on properly. Then his head lolled to the left and she thought he was going to tumble over. She ended up putting his right arm around her shoulder, the pajama top over his head, then working each arm. By the time she was done, she was actually breathing hard.

But being winded wasn't half as bad as the other thing. The tragic truth was—she was turned on. Terribly. Achingly. Every touch of his skin stirred something deep inside her, a longing that had been there forever. Dormant so long, now awakening with a fierceness that made her giddy.

She stood, took him by the shoulders and laid him down on the couch. She picked up his legs, straightened them, and put them on the couch, too. His cowboy boots came off next, after a hell of a fight.

Okay. So the only thing left was the bottoms.

She tugged the legs of his jeans, but nothing happened. She tried again. Nada. She'd have to attack this from a different angle.

Moving up, she took hold of his jeans at the hips. As she pulled on the well-worn material, she saw that his boxers were coming down, too. Oh, dear.

His belly button was perfect. The dark hair on his body was perfect. His muscles…she had a whole new respect for athletics.

She meant to just pull his shorts up. That's all. But suddenly, she was leaning over him, her hands on his belly. Her lips so close to his chest that she couldn't help herself. She kissed him. Kissed him on his chest. She inhaled his scent, which was masculine and sharp, not quite hidden by the aroma of beer.

How she'd loved him. All those years. Silently, passionately, she'd given her heart to him, and he didn't know it. Now she knew she could never tell him. Not after today.

She kissed him once more as she whispered goodbye. It wasn't going to work out. Not ever. He was going to go off and live his glamorous life, and she was going to stay here, being Emily. Good old Emily. She prayed she'd meet someone nice someday.

She kissed the tip of his chin. Just as she was rising, his hand landed on her neck, scaring her to death. She gasped. His eyes opened. She tried to get away, but he held her steady with surprising strength. His gaze focused, and she didn't think he was drunk anymore.

He pulled her to him, right to his lips, right to a kiss.

To a kiss that made the rest of the universe disappear.

His tongue teased her, his heat warmed her insides, and he kissed her the way she'd always wanted to be kissed. Perfect, *perfect*.

Of course he was drunk, she knew that. But that didn't matter too much, did it? He knew it was her, after all. He'd called her Em about ten times.

He pulled her down farther, until she was on the couch, too, and then she was lying next to him, as close as a lover.

He shifted to his side and so did she. He broke the kiss, and when she opened her eyes, she saw his eyes were closed. A sharp stab of disappointment hit her where she was most vulnerable. But then he sighed and kissed her once more. A long, languid exploration. His hand moved to her chest and she gasped as he cupped her breast.

This was it. The night she'd wished for. It wasn't the way she'd hoped it would be. But then, what else could she expect? He probably wouldn't even remember this in the morning. Which was for the best. If he were awake, alert, he'd realize that she'd

never done this before, and she wasn't at all prepared to answer the inevitable questions the revelation would spur.

He moved his mouth to her neck and his lips
and tongue tickled her deliciously. His fingers
found her nipple, and he squeezed it gently. Heat
filled her, pooling at the junction of her thighs. She
pushed herself against him and he slipped his leg
between hers. As he moved back to her lips, he
brought his leg up so that as she moved her hips
he rubbed against her. It was almost too much.

"Oh, baby," he whispered. "You feel so
good."

It wasn't love. It wasn't even honest lust, but
one thing she'd learned after all these years was
how to pretend. So tonight, she'd use her skills of
make-believe, and when he touched her, it would
be reverent, and when he looked into her eyes, he'd
see nothing but beauty. And when he called her
name, it would be out of love.

He moved his hand from her breast, and a second later she felt his fingers on her leg, scant
inches below the hem of her nightshirt. Then, with
cunning ease, he slipped under her shirt and moved
his hand slowly up her thigh.

She closed her eyes, focusing all her attention
on the riot of sensations in her body. The anticipation, the ache, the need. She wanted him so desperately.

His fingers trailed over her hip then up her tummy, tickling her, making her shiver. Then she felt him touch the slight patch of curly hair between her legs. A second later, she cried out as his fingers went inside her.

"So hot," he whispered. "So wet."

For a moment she lay perfectly still, immobilized by his bold caress. Then she moved her hips. It wasn't as if she had a choice. Her need had taken over the controls and she was helpless to do anything but surrender.

He teased her with his fingers. Rubbing her in small circles, slowly at first, then faster. She abandoned herself to the intense sensations as they built and built until her muscles had grown taut. Before she went over the edge, she had to do one thing.

She moved her hand down to his open fly, to his boxer shorts. Her own pleasure gave her courage and she touched him. Hot, thick, so hard it made her gasp. To have him inside her was all she wanted. All she'd ever wanted.

She opened her legs and he moaned. He found her mouth again as he turned them both so she was underneath him. With his free hand he lifted her nightshirt until it bunched above her chest. She helped him slip it over her head. Then he lowered his hand and caressed her once more, finding the precise spot that took her breath away. His body moved against her, rubbed her, making her need build to excruciating heights.

"Scott," she whispered.

"Baby," he whispered back. "You feel so good."

"I know you won't remember this. But I will. I love you. I've always loved you."

"I know," he said as his fingers slipped out of her. He pushed down his pants, but she couldn't see him. Not in this position. So she closed her eyes as she readied to take him inside her.

"Make love to me," she said, gripping the side of the couch. "I want you so much." She felt him at her entrance, and her body fairly melted with want. He paused and she pushed her hips up, but still, he held back.

"Scott," she said, her voice high and strained with desire.

His gaze locked onto hers, holding her captive. He kissed her softly on the lips, then moved his mouth to her ear, nibbling on the lobe, nipping her playfully. As he pushed inside her, he whispered one word.

"Cathy."

Chapter Ten

The pain woke him. Throbbing in his temples, throbbing so bad it felt as if his head were being squeezed in a vise. He forced one eye open, then closed it immediately. The room was sunny and bright and it nearly killed him.

Something else wasn't right. He couldn't move his left elbow. He didn't remember putting anything in his bed. Deciding not to worry about it now, he rolled to his right. And fell. Hard.

He groaned as nerve cell after nerve cell punished him for a lifetime of mistakes. So he was dead, eh? And this was hell. All he could do was lie there for a good long while, wondering if he was going to throw up. He closed both eyes and said a little prayer to the god of hangovers.

The next thing he knew, something tickled his face. He swiped at it, but it came back. He opened his eyes and gasped. A cat stared at him, inches

from his face. Stared at him as if he were a particularly large mouse.

Scott jolted up, holding the sides of his head.
What the hell? He was wearing blue pajama tops
and his boxer shorts. The shorts he remembered.
The top was completely unfamiliar. So was the
room. No, wait. Those were bookcases. There was
that fishbowl with the fake fish. *Emily.*

He was at Emily's apartment. How he'd gotten
there, he had no idea. In fact, the last thing he
remembered was sitting at the Long Horn. Feeling
sorry for himself. Drinking. Oh, man, had he been
drinking.

Emily must have taken him home. Given him
the pajama tops. Made the bed. Good old Em.
She'd come through again. Even after…he tried to
remember yesterday. Oh, yeah. He'd almost kissed
her. Almost blown it with his best friend. But she
hadn't let it come between them.

Struggling to his feet, he found his jeans wadded
up at the end of the couch. His boots on the floor.
His shirt on top of his boots. The smell of stale
beer wafted up from his clothes, and he had to stay
real still so he didn't lose whatever was in his
stomach.

Finally the danger subsided and he was able to
get his things and head for the bathroom. A
shower. God, he wanted a shower more than any-

thing in his whole life. More than peace in our time. Even more than the job at ESPN.

He closed the door with his foot, then turned on the water. For a moment he debated going through Emily's drawers, but the fur on his teeth outweighed the ethical problem. He hit pay dirt third drawer down. A brand-new, never-opened toothbrush. His hands shook as he tried to find the little strip that would open the cellophane. Finally he just ripped the box apart.

Before he got the toothpaste, he turned on the water in the shower to let it get nice and hot. Then he stripped, and standing naked, he brushed his teeth really, really well as he searched for the second most important thing in the universe: aspirin.

The bottle was right there, in the middle of the bathroom cabinet. After he rinsed his mouth, he popped down four then eased himself into the shower. The hot water was nothing less than a miracle. It pounded his shoulders, sluiced down his back, washed away his sins. Closing his eyes turned out to be a mistake as vertigo sent him reeling.

He'd never had a hangover like this. Not much of a drinker, he usually nursed a beer or two and that was it. He must have downed a fifth of tequila to pay so dearly this morning.

The most troubling thing wasn't his head, although if that didn't get better soon he was going to consider the emergency room. No, the most troubling thing was the fact that he couldn't remember most of the night.

The bar. Alan. Cathy. Cathy! That's right. She'd been there. He'd told her he couldn't see her anymore. Yeah, yeah, that's right. He'd told her and she'd been real upset. Or was that Hope? Hope? Had she been there, too?

He leaned his head on the cool tile. What a mess. His life was going down the toilet, and he had no idea how to fix it. At least the Cathy situation was under control. He'd hated to do it to her, but ending things was for the best. No way he could commit to anything right now. And the last thing he wanted to do was string her along.

He'd stick with Emily. She was exactly the friend he needed. If she wasn't still mad at him for that lughead move yesterday.

He got the bar of soap and began to wash. As he did, he found himself getting aroused. Which was amazing, considering the way he felt. But he kept thinking about what must have been a dream. About Emily. Flashes of the dream kept popping up. Kissing her. Touching her soft skin. Her hand on him.

Whoa. He closed his eyes, forcing his thoughts to behave. They flatly refused. In fact, they took him places he'd never gone before.

Emily. Why hadn't he seen it before? She'd been

right there, and he'd never given her a second thought—not that way, at least. But the dream had opened his eyes. He'd always thought she was attractive, and he'd felt sure she would have been snapped up by some lucky guy by now. Was it possible that guy could be him?

No. He wasn't going to be here. Besides, Emily didn't see him that way. He'd found that out yesterday.

The smart thing to do was finish up here, get dressed and go home. Sleep off this weirdness. Emily and him? Wouldn't happen. Couldn't happen. He needed her too much right now.

But it wouldn't hurt anything to have a few unchaste thoughts about her, would it? Here, in private? No one needed to know. No one…

Oh, God.

EMILY HEARD THE SHOWER turn off. She couldn't believe she'd let him get to her like this. Her eyes were puffy and red, her face blotchy, her nerves on edge. Why did it hurt so much? She'd known he didn't want her. Alcohol couldn't change that. He'd been drunk, not brainwashed.

She'd relived the horrible moment over and over. Winced over how she'd touched him, and worse, how she'd let him touch her. It was the stuff nightmares were made of. She knew with absolute certainty that this particular nightmare would haunt her forever. All she wanted was to take it back. Take back the night, take back her wishes.

She certainly never wanted to see Scott again. God, she was so humiliated! At least she knew he was too much of a gentleman to mention this to anyone. She'd keep it quiet to her grave. Fresh tears filled her eyes and she wiped them away angrily with the back of her hands. No more! She'd cried herself to sleep, and even that hadn't happened until about an hour ago. She was exhausted, the weight of her shame making it hard to lift her head.

But he needed a ride home.

She could tell him to call Cathy, but the ramifications were too horrible to contemplate. Cathy would lord it over her, rub her face in it. She was too tired to go through any of that. So she'd drive Scott to his car, and then she'd come home, take a long, hot bath, and consider her options.

She could become a nun, only she wasn't Catholic. She could become a lesbian, only she'd probably fall in love with the wrong woman. She could go back to her quiet life, teaching, loving her friends and her family, doing all the things she'd always done, only now she wouldn't wake up to thoughts of Scott. She wouldn't daydream about him when the kids were taking tests. She wouldn't think about him when she watched television, or dream of him when she slept. The scary part was the thought of the Scott-sized hole that would leave in her life. How could another man fill that? How could she learn to live so incomplete?

She swallowed the lump in her throat and picked up her foundation. As she applied the pale makeup to her face, she stared at herself in the mirror. What she saw was a joke. A big, fat joke of a woman. It broke her heart.

SCOTT RAISED HIS HAND to knock on Emily's door, but he didn't. She was probably sleeping. Maybe he should just wait until she got up on her own. Who knows how late he'd kept her up?

He felt better, thank God. The shower had done wonders, the aspirin even more. And the coffee he'd made felt damn fine going down. He'd like to bring Emily a cup, but he didn't know how she liked it.

He didn't know a million things about her. After his revelation in the shower, he'd realized something else. His relationship with Emily was all one-sided. She was always there for him, but what had he done for her? Nothing, except make a pass at her, and then add insult to injury by having her rescue him from a night of stupidity and alcohol.

She was probably mad at him. Hell, she ought to be mad at him. He'd been a jerk. A monumental jerk. But he had hope. She had come to the bar, right? She could have told him to go to hell. So that must mean the friendship was intact. Or at least, not completely shattered.

He raised his hand again. Knocked so lightly that if she was asleep she wouldn't hear him. But if she was awake…he needed to apologize. The sooner the better.

"Yes?"

She was up. He couldn't tell her mood, though. Not from the one word. "I've made coffee. Can I bring you a cup?"

"No."

Uh-oh. That didn't sound good. She was mad. No doubt about it. "Uh, can I get you some juice or something?"

He jerked back as her door swung open. She was awake, and she looked as though she wanted to bash him in the nose.

"Let's go," she said, pushing past him.

"Em?"

She didn't turn. Didn't acknowledge him in any way. What the heck had he done last night? Why had he gotten drunk? He knew it didn't solve anything. And it just might have ruined something he valued very highly.

She went to the door and held it open while she looked back at him. "Are you coming?"

He nodded, but as he headed toward her, it occurred to him that she'd changed. Not because she was mad, but because he didn't see her the same way as before. Now, all he could see was the shine of her hair, the pale beauty of her skin. Her full lips, her full breasts. She was a voluptuous woman, ripe for the plucking. Fool! Damn fool for not seeing what was right in front of his nose.

Before he reached her, she walked out. He shut the door behind them, and by that time, she was halfway to the parking lot. As he hurried to catch up, she didn't acknowledge him at all. She just went straight to her car and got behind the wheel.

He smiled as he sat in the passenger seat. But the look she gave him withered his grin. She turned the key, backed out of her parking place and headed for the street. All without a word. Without a glimmer of anything but anger.

Three blocks from the bar, Scott couldn't stand it any longer. "Emily. What's wrong?"

She gave him a scathing look for an answer. It made him feel like hell but it didn't help anything.

"It's because I was drunk, right? I know. It was really stupid of me. I never get drunk. I was feeling sorry for myself and—"

She turned the corner so fast he nearly flew into her lap. He straightened and gripped the seat, hanging on for dear life.

"I didn't mean to drag you into it," he said, half-fearing she would open his door on the next turn and toss him out of the car. Thankfully, he had his seat belt on. But he wasn't sure that would be enough to stop her.

"I mean it, Em," he said, his heart galloping in his chest as she turned another corner at the speed of light. "I should have just called a taxi. I didn't want you to see me like that."

She roared into the Long Horn's parking lot and came to a jolting stop by his GTO.

He turned to face her. To take his medicine. "Please accept my apology. I didn't mean to—"

"It's always about you, isn't it?"

He nodded. "Yeah, I know. I was thinking about that this morning. I really have been selfish, and I'm sorry for that."

"Oh, who cares. Just go."

"Em—"

"I said, go. Get the hell out."

He undid his seat belt and opened the door, his face hot with confusion and shame. This was Emily. The one person he'd always been able to count on. And now, he'd blown it with her. Blown it big time.

She stepped on the gas even before the door shut all the way. He watched her speed dangerously around a Camaro, then onto the street. He raised his hand to stop her, but she was gone.

He'd really done it this time. He'd chased her away with his selfishness, with his stupidity. The irony wasn't lost on him. He'd only just realized he wanted her to be much more than a friend, and now she wasn't even that.

Perfect. Just effing perfect.

EMILY COULDN'T STAND IT anymore. The phone hadn't stopped ringing all afternoon and it was driving her crazy. She leaned over the edge of her bed and unclipped the phone from the jack. The silence bathed her like sunshine, and she smiled for the first time that day.

Her caller ID told her Scott had phoned three times, Hope five, Lily four, Julia twice, and even Zoey, Sam, and Emily's mother had tried to reach her. She didn't care. She didn't want to talk to a living soul. Not today. Maybe never again.

All she cared about right now was the bag of Oreo cookies on her lap.

What was the use of being skinny if all it brought was more heartache? Besides, it was clear to her now that she could lose all the weight in the world, but she'd still be Emily inside. How long had she believed that once she lost weight, everything would be perfect? A lie, that's what that was. A lie she'd told herself so she could go on with her day. So she could believe that somehow, some way, Scott could be hers.

Well, she didn't want him anymore. In fact, she couldn't even fathom why she'd wanted him in the first place. The jerk. He hadn't even noticed that she was thinner. All he cared about was his precious career and *Cathy*. He could have her. Emily didn't care. She'd send them a damn toaster as a wedding present.

She plucked another cookie from the bag and she didn't bother to open it. She popped the whole thing in her mouth and chewed with a vengeance.

The TV show she'd been watching ended, and for the life of her she couldn't remember what it had been. The commercials, with all their skinny women, mocked her. Diet plans one minute, fast-food ads the next. It was all a joke. A horrible, tragic joke. A world that celebrated food and idolized thinness. Well, ha-ha. Very amusing.

She gulped down some milk, then ate another cookie. A movie came up next. A romance. She changed the channel. Wrestling. That was more like it. She'd never seen a wrestling match before, but right off the bat she could relate. It was almost too easy to picture Scott in the ring, being pummeled by the blonde with the forty-inch biceps.

But even that pleasure dimmed in only a few minutes. She turned the channel again, flipping through the network stations then the cable shows. Nothing appealed to her.

It was as if she'd lost her taste for life. Even the Oreo cookies, once valued friends, had turned on her. She was eating them out of spite, not enjoyment. She put the bag down. Boo took the opportunity to crawl into her lap. The minute she started petting him he purred like a little motor boat. His eyes closed in complete contentment.

Impossibly, hot tears came to her eyes. Impossible because she'd truly believed she'd cried herself out. She certainly felt empty inside. Mostly, though, she just felt stupid. So much of her life wasted on castles in the sand. On dreams that could never come true.

She scratched Boo's chin, then moved him next to her so that she could curl up around him. In a final act of pure grief, she pulled the covers over her head and buried her face in the pillow. Her sobs came from the deepest part of her. From her very soul.

Scott had been her reason. What was she going to do now?

Chapter Eleven

Scott rubbed the side of his head, wishing the remnants of his hangover would leave already. It had been a horrible day, mostly because Emily hadn't answered his phone calls. He'd also felt like hell, but he figured he deserved that. The store, thank goodness, had been unusually quiet, and he'd let Miguel take over for the afternoon.

He rang Hope's doorbell again, wondering whether she was at Emily's. A few seconds later, he had his answer. She swung the door open without asking who it was. That was Sheridan, though. Trusting. Too trusting.

"Oh!"

"Hi, Hope."

"What are you doing here?"

"I came to talk. If you have a few minutes."

"Sure." She stepped back, ushering him inside her apartment. The living room was as dramatic as Hope herself. Oriental in theme, black lacquer and scarlet the predominant colors. She had a low, modern black couch, a black lacquer coffee table, a futon chair, and she had Asian prints on the walls. It smelled good, like some exotic flower.

Hope nodded toward the couch, and he saw she wasn't wearing shoes. Her toenails were bright red, matching the pillows on the couch. Her outfit was the only thing that didn't go with the decor. She wore jeans so old they were torn at the knee, and an *X-Files* T-shirt. He sat, surprised at how comfortable the couch was.

"What's up?" Hope sat on the futon cushions, curling her legs under her.

"Have you spoken to Emily today?"

"No. I called though. I thought she was with you."

He shook his head. "I left this morning."

Her right brow raised.

"I slept on the couch. She found me last night at the Long Horn. I was drunk. She took me home."

"I see," Hope said, although her voice had gone from friendly to frosty. "What happened after you got to her house?"

He grimaced. Moved his gaze to the bonsai plant on the side table. "I don't know. I don't remember. But I sure did something to make her furious with me."

"Furious?"

He nodded. "She hardly said a word to me this morning. And when I tried to apologize she told me to get the hell out of her car."

Both of Hope's brows rose on that one. "My, my. So she kicked you out on your butt, eh?"

"What does that mean?"

Hope sighed as she shook her head. "Nothing."

"Bull. Come on, Hope. Tell me what's going on."

"I can't."

"You're the one that got me in trouble, you know. All that cryptic nonsense at the store. Why don't you just tell me what you meant? Maybe give me a chance to make things right."

She stared at him for a long time. He knew she was debating telling him the truth, and if he could have thought of the perfect thing to say to convince her to speak, he would have said it. As it was, he had to settle for looking earnest. At least he hoped he looked earnest and not deranged.

His hopes were dashed by the shake of her head. "I can't. I want to, but I can't. It's not for me to do without Emily's permission."

He cursed silently. "Will you go talk to her then? At least try and find out what I did that made her so crazy. I thought it was because I was drunk, but now…I think it might have been about what happened yesterday."

"Something else happened?"

He nodded. "I almost— I made a mistake. I wasn't thinking."

"What did you do?"

Now it was his turn to wonder whether he should tell all. Hope was Emily's good friend. But what if Emily wanted to keep things private? What if, by telling Hope, he did even more damage to their relationship? "I'm sorry, Hope. I don't think I can."

She nodded. "I understand."

"I know you do. Because you have her best interests at heart."

"What do you have at heart?"

"She's important to me, Hope. She really is. I don't want to lose her."

"Why? You've got Cathy."

He shook his head. "Not anymore."

"What?"

"I ended things between us last night. At least, I hope I did."

"You can't remember that?"

"Nope. But I'm pretty sure that's what happened." He ran a hand through his hair. "I don't know. That's what's making me nuts. I don't remember anything."

"I'll see what I can do," she said. "But I'll tell you right now, my priority is Emily."

"Mine, too."

She stood up. "Go home. You look like hell. I'll talk to you tomorrow."

He got to his feet, winced as his aching head protested the sudden move, then went over to Hope. He took her hand in his. She was so tiny. A miniature person with really red nails. "Thanks. I mean it."

"Don't thank me yet. I might not be doing you any favors."

"But you'll take care of her. That's enough to be grateful for."

She studied him again, searching his face, for what, he wasn't sure. But when her gaze came back to meet his, her mouth softened into a smile. "Go home."

He leaned down and kissed her cheek. "Thanks."

Hope nodded. Despite everything, she had to admit Scott was a decent guy. Although they'd never been close, she'd known him as long as Emily had, and she'd certainly written about him enough.

As she walked him to the door, she thought about all the years she'd spent covering sports for the local newspaper. Scott was the biggest thing to hit this town since the days of the Texas Rangers.

"You'll call?" he asked.

She nodded. "As soon as I know anything."

He squeezed her hand, then walked out to his GTO. She closed the door as she heard the engine rev. It was time to make a decision. One that would affect a lot of people.

First, though, she needed to give Emily another try. Moving to the phone, she hit speed dial 1. She counted twelve rings before she hung up. That swung the vote.

She sat down on the couch, still carrying the phone. Then she made four phone calls. One to Sam, one to Zoey, one to Lily and one to Julia. Each time she got an answering machine, but that didn't bother her. Her message was short. "Code Red," she said. "Emily's in trouble." That was it. No explanations were needed.

A Code Red was the most important part of The Girlfriends' pact. It was only to be used in the most dire circumstances, when nothing else would save the day. Lily and Julia would know to go right to Emily's as soon as they got the message. Sam would call from San Francisco, and Zoey would call from Houston, and they'd both be on the next plane if necessary. In the meantime, Hope was the line of first defense. She went to her junk drawer and piled all the warranties, coupons, matchbooks and tape on the counter. Then she took the entire drawer out and turned it upside down. Five keys were taped to the bottom. She took the one marked Emily.

By the time she got to Emily's apartment, it was

four-fifteen. Tomorrow was a school day, so odds were Em was home.

She knocked on the door. No answer. She knocked again. Louder. This time she heard a faint, "Go away."

"Not a chance, darlin'" Hope said, pulling the key out of her pocket. She was inside in two seconds. And there was Emily, on the couch. It was a pathetic sight. A crumbled Oreo box lay on one side of her feet, a bag of sour cream and chives potato chips on the other. Emily hadn't brushed her hair, put on makeup, nothing. In fact, she had on a nightshirt that must have been saved from the Crimean War. It was so old, there were patches that were completely transparent.

"Hope, go home."

"Like that's gonna happen?"

"I mean it. I don't want to talk."

"Tough titties. I do." She tossed her purse onto the coffee table and sat down heavily next to her friend. "What are we watching?"

"I don't know."

"You don't know? George Clooney in scrubs didn't give you a clue?"

Emily gave her a look that would have daunted a Hell's Angel. But Hope didn't even blink.

"I'm going to stay until you tell me."

"Then you'd better go get your suitcases, 'cause I'm not saying a word."

"You think that scares me?"

Emily jammed a piece of chocolate into her mouth.

"Oh, that hurts. You're eating at me? Well, honey, I hate to have to say it, but those calories aren't going to end up on *my* hips."

"Who cares?"

"Not me. I love you no matter what. I think you're gorgeous and wonderful, and you don't need to change a thing. You're the one—"

"Stop. I don't need a lecture, Hope."

"That wasn't a lecture. It was a statement of fact. If you choose to hear it as a lecture, that's too darn bad."

"Why'd you come over? To make me completely insane?"

Hope shook her head. "You do that quite nicely without me."

"Thank God, you didn't call anyone else. I couldn't deal with more than one of you."

As if in response to the statement, someone knocked on the door. Emily turned to Hope with a cry of dismay. A moment later, Lily walked in. "What's going on."

"You didn't," Emily said.

"I did."

"Why!"

Hope looked at the discarded food packages on

the floor, then at the crumbs on Emily's ancient T-shirt. "Why do you think?"

"Can't you guys understand that I don't want to talk about it? I'm humiliated enough without having to tell the whole world."

"Since when are The Girlfriends the whole world?" Lily asked, plopping down on the big chair.

"Are all of you coming?"

"I don't know about Sam and Zoey. It depends on how stubborn you're going to be."

Emily put her head in her hands. "I hate you all," she mumbled.

"We know, honey," Lily said.

"You can hate us all you want," Hope added. "But we're not leaving until you spill."

Emily looked up again, and the expression on her face nearly broke Hope's heart. Emily was the nicest person she'd ever met. And that was no exaggeration. Em was generous to a fault, and never asked for anything for herself. She was never happier than when she was doing something for someone else.

"What did he do?" Lily asked Hope. "I assume this is about Scott, right?"

Hope nodded.

"He didn't do anything," Emily said.

"Liar."

"He didn't. Nothing that was his fault."

"Then why did you tell him to get the hell out of your car?" Hope asked.

Emily's back straightened. "Did you talk to him?"

"Yep. He came over about two hours ago."

"What did he say?"

"I don't want to talk about it," Hope said, mimicking Emily's words.

Emily turned to Lily. "Will you do something, please?"

"What?"

"I don't know. Slap her."

Lily turned to Hope. "Consider yourself slapped."

"This isn't funny!"

"What isn't funny, Em?"

"Oh, crap."

"Yeah," Lily said, nodding in agreement. "It is crappy to have people love you so much they won't let you wallow in self-pity."

"There's nothing wrong with self-pity," Emily said.

Hope leaned over and took Emily's hand. "Then why do you work so hard at making sure none of us indulge?"

"That's different."

Hope smiled. "My ass."

Another knock on the door. Emily sighed. "Come in, Julia."

The door opened. Julia hadn't come empty-handed. She held a bottle of wine in one hand and a bag of miniature peeled carrots in the other. "What's happened?"

"We don't know yet," Lily said.

"Scott did something terrible," Hope added.

"Oh, no." Julia went straight to the kitchen, but in two minutes flat she was back holding a tray filled with wineglasses, carrots and low-fat crackers. As soon as she put it on the coffee table, she disappeared again, returning with the wine, a corkscrew and a jar of peanut butter. She sat on the floor, poured herself a glass of wine, took a spoonful of peanut butter, and looked from Lily to Hope to Emily. "What did he do?"

"I told you. He didn't do anything. It was my fault, not his."

"What was your fault?" Julia asked, licking the peanut butter like a lollipop.

"Oh, for God's sake. Please—"

"It's not like we want the information to torture you with it." Lily leaned forward, her face filled with concern. "Kiddo, this is it. The reason for The Girlfriends. The whole purpose is to be able to confess the worst to people who love you completely. No matter what. We're on your side, remember?"

Emily sat very still for a long minute. Then she sat back, dusted some crumbs from her T-shirt and shook her head in resignation. "So where're Zoey and Sam?"

Hope felt the tension in her stomach ease. It was going to be all right.

Emily looked at her friends, at their wonderful, beautiful faces. They did love her unconditionally, and that was huge. It was maybe the single most important thing in her life. Her friends, who'd walk through fire for her, who'd take a bullet. Who'd understand why her heart was shattered.

"Yesterday afternoon," she began, "Scott came over and we were having this great talk. We really made a connection, you know? It was as if he was seeing me for the first time. He touched my face—" Tears welled and her throat closed. She waited a moment, then figured she could talk again. "He leaned over to kiss me. And then he stopped. Pulled back. As if he'd just awakened and found himself about to kiss a frog."

Emily held up her hand, not wanting their consolation yet. If she hesitated, she'd never tell them the rest. "Then last night I picked him up from the bar. He was drunk as hell, and he couldn't even stand up straight. But after a while, he sobered up a little. And then, we, uh—" Again the tears formed. But if she waited for them to stop, she'd never finish. "We kissed. It was amazing. I knew it wasn't love, but it was what I'd asked for. It was my one night with Scott. Only—"

Hope took her hand and squeezed it. Lily got the box of tissue from the floor and handed it to her. Julia scooted closer and rested her head on Emily's leg.

"Only, when we...when we started to make love...he looked me right in the eye, and called me Cathy."

"Oh, my God," Julia whispered. Hope groaned as if she'd been wounded. Lily flinched. Emily let the tears flow, praying that telling her friends was the right thing to do. That it would ease her pain and her humiliation.

Hope squeezed her hand again. "Emily, I know it must have been hard to go through, but I don't think it's the end of the world."

"I know," Emily said. "It's just the end of my dream."

"No. That's what I mean. It's not. He was drunk. Really drunk. When he came by this afternoon, he had no recollection of last night. None. He thought you were mad because he was drunk, and he couldn't stand it. He came over, begging me to make sure you were all right."

"But—"

"She's right," Lily said, cutting off Emily's protest before she could even say it. "You can't let one night ruin everything you've worked for."

"Oh, no. I'm not going to torture myself anymore. This is it. I weigh what I weigh. The end. No more starvation. I won't do it.''

"That's fine," Julia said. "You don't have to. As long as you're comfortable with yourself—''

Emily burst out laughing. "Comfortable?''

Lily nodded. "Screw Scott. The best thing about the last few weeks has been how happy and proud you've been. You've never looked more beautiful. You carried yourself with such pride, it's a wonder to me the entire male population of Sheridan hasn't lined up at your door.''

"And frankly," Hope said, her voice very low and calm, "I think that dream of yours was pretty crummy. One night. Please. You deserve so much more.''

"You do, Em," Julia said. "Scott may have been the dream guy, but the truth is, you deserve someone real. Someone who can appreciate you for all you are.''

Emily wiped her eyes, but it didn't stop the tears. She let go of Hope's hand and got off the couch. She couldn't even excuse herself as she ran to the bathroom. After she shut the door, she leaned over the sink, crying as she'd never cried before. But then she caught sight of her reflection. She swallowed as she stood up straighter. Her eyes were puffy as hell, her nose was running and red, her hair was something out of a horror movie, but the thing was, she didn't hate the woman in the mirror. She didn't hate her at all. The woman in the mirror was actually pretty wonderful. Strong. Capable. So what if she wasn't model-thin? Who cared? In the past few weeks she had taken a lot of steps forward. She was becoming the person she'd always wanted to be.

She wasn't going to let Scott take that all away. Scott or no Scott, she was going to keep on with her plan. Keep on getting stronger. And she'd find a new dream. It wouldn't be for one night, either. She deserved more. She deserved a lifetime love, and damned if she wasn't going to get it.

Chapter Twelve

Sara Wilding leaned into Scott's office. "There's someone here to see you."

He put down his pen as he stood up behind his desk. *Emily.* It was Emily, it had to be. All his phone calls over the past five days had finally gotten through to her. He ran a quick hand through his hair, then headed for the door.

His smile died as he caught sight of his visitor. Cathy. Oh, man. He wasn't prepared for her. She didn't look happy. Her face, so perfectly made-up, looked stiff to him. Especially around her mouth. "Hi, Cathy."

She turned and gave him a grin that made him stop in his tracks. It wasn't the smile of a woman who'd been dumped. That was Cathy's "let's do lunch at the Shady Lane Motel" smile. "I'm mad at you," she said, going into an instant pout.

"You are?"

"Why haven't you called me? It's been five whole days."

"I, uh...you, uh, want to come on back?"

She raised her brow suggestively and preceded him to his office. He fought down his panic, trying to think what to do. She waited by the door and, when he walked past her, she pushed it closed. Her hands went to her hips. "Well?"

He went to his desk. Picked up his clipboard, then put it down again. Had he broken up with her? Or, like that dream about Emily, had it all been a product of his drunken delusions? "About the other night," he said lamely, trying like hell to act as if he was in control, when in fact all he wanted to do was bolt past her and run right out of the store.

She looked down, blushing a little. "Now, don't hold that against me. I'm not used to tequila."

"No, no. I wouldn't hold it against you. I don't drink, either. But..."

"But?" She came toward him slowly, her hips swinging provocatively, her gaze hungry.

"Cathy, I don't know how to say this, really."

She stopped. Her brows furrowed. "Say what?"

"We talked the other night. About us."

She didn't say anything.

He took a deep breath. "About how I'm not going to be here very long, and how, uh, we... I mean the two of us... How it's not going to, um, you know, work out."

Her shoulders sagged. "It wasn't a dream?" she whispered, more to herself than him.

"I don't think so."

"I'm embarrassed. I thought— I can't quite remember…"

"Listen, it's been great seeing you again. Really great. But I just don't think it's the smart thing to do right now. I've got the store, and the ESPN job isn't over yet and—"

"Emily."

"What?"

"You've got Emily. I didn't forget that part."

"Huh?"

"I've seen the way you look at her."

His mouth was open, but no words came out. Finally he shook his head, not knowing how to respond.

"Oh, well," she said, her smile back, but not the same. The seductiveness had been replaced by a sort of desperate sadness he'd have given anything not to see. "*C'est la vie.*"

"I think you're great, Cathy. I do."

"Yeah. Right." She went back to the door and gripped the knob. "I'll see you around."

"Cathy!"

She didn't stop. She walked out the door and closed it behind her.

Scott slumped against his desk. What a prince he was. He'd hurt two women he cared about. And he'd been home less than a month.

At least with Cathy, he knew he'd done the right thing, even if it hadn't been easy. But Emily…

What had Cathy said about her? She'd seen the way he looked at Em. Did he look a certain way? Before he could stop himself, he picked up the phone and dialed her number. It rang once, then her voice, bright as a new penny, told him to leave a message.

"Em, please. I need you." He hung up. What if she didn't call back? What if he'd blown it completely? Now he didn't even have Cathy. No, that wasn't the issue. He hadn't been kidding with his message. He needed her. Living in Sheridan without her friendship was so bleak he couldn't think about it. Now that he'd found her again, he didn't want to let her go.

Women. What a concept. He didn't understand the first thing about them. He never used to put Em in that category, but now, she was the most confusing one of all.

He put his hand on the phone again, but he didn't pick it up. Instead, he left his office and went into the break room. Gretchen Foley was there. Good. He'd seen her a while ago, waiting for Bobby to finish work. She straddled one of the folding chairs, leaning over the table reading a magazine. She was young, but from what he'd seen of Gretchen, she knew more than her years could explain.

"Hey, Mr. Dillon."

"Scott."

She smiled at him and he was reminded of Cathy when she'd been seventeen. Gretchen was going to break a lot of hearts.

"Mind if I join you?"

"No." She flipped her long blond hair behind her shoulder and stared at him with big blue eyes.

"I've got a question."

"Shoot."

"If Bobby got you mad, really mad, what would he have to do to make it up to you?"

She nibbled her upper lip for a moment. "It depends on what kind of mad I was."

"Pardon?"

"There's like mad because a guy doesn't do what he's supposed to, like not showing up at the library or something. Then there's mad because a guy is walking on your heart."

"And that one's worse?"

"Oh, yeah. That one can be the end."

"So, okay. Let's say that's the mad we're talking about. What would Bobby have to do to make things right?"

"Well, like, he'd have to apologize."

"Okay."

"And, he'd, like have to show me that he was real sorry."

"How?"

She shrugged. "I don't know. Probably by like coming over and all. And, you know, showing people he liked me. Putting his arm around me and holding hands. I don't know. Something like that. He'd need to like spend some money, too. Not just pizza, but a real dinner, and maybe a movie or something."

"I see. One more question, Gretchen. What if Bobby didn't know what you were mad about?"

She laughed. "Like it ever happens any other way?"

Scott leaned forward. "You mean, that happens a lot?"

"All the time."

"Thanks, Gretchen."

"Sure." She hit him with the smile again. "Um, is Bobby almost finished?"

The boy still had another hour on the clock, but to thank Gretchen, he was going to let him go home now. Scott would clock him out at four, when he left the store. After that? Scott was going to have to do some, like, apologizing and all.

EMILY PUT BOO'S FOOD DOWN, and watched as the orange cat scarfed down the liver and chicken. Ugh. She headed back to the counter where she was chopping veggies for her own dinner. Brown rice, steamed broccoli, cauliflower, carrots and mushrooms, and to top it all off, three ounces of chicken breast. She grimaced, but it wasn't really so bad. She liked everything she was making, but she couldn't stop her head from picturing lasagna and cheeseburgers. This weekend, she'd have something sinful. It was something to look forward to.

She picked up her knife, but she didn't cut right away. She was trying to think of something else in her life that she was looking forward to. Oh, man. Having food as her only reward was exactly what she didn't want to do. Something had to change.

She left her dinner on the counter and pulled the phone book out of the utility cabinet. A few seconds later, she was on the phone with a very nice lady at the Y. A catalogue would be put in the mail tomorrow, and oh, yes, they had lots of activities for singles.

Singles. Em thought about the word as she hung up the phone. She'd never cared one whit that she was single. At twenty-six, it was appropriate. Gone were the days of getting hitched right out of high school. She had life to live! Things to do! Who'd want to get saddled with a husband before thirty? And once there were kids, forget it. She was single, and proud of it.

Except for…

No. No more thinking about *him*.

It had been six days. Six days to adjust to her new way of living. To see the world without Scott in the picture. So far? It pretty much sucked. But it was only six days, right?

She caught her reflection in the toaster. She wasn't so bad. A little chubby, but also healthier than she'd ever been before. She pushed a loose tendril of hair behind her ear. Her makeup still looked good after a full day teaching. That was new. She'd hardly ever worn makeup, and if she did, it was usually just a little blush and a little mascara. But since...that day, she'd made a real effort to look as good as she could. Lily and Hope had taken her shopping and they'd insisted she stop buying clothes that were shapeless and hid her body.

People had commented, too. At school. At Zeke's Place on Tuesday. Denise Knight had been behind her at the ATM, and she'd gone overboard telling Emily how wonderful she looked.

If only she felt wonderful. If only the ache inside her would go away. She felt as if she'd been broken. Thrown off a shelf like some piece of pottery, a vital piece of her shattered beyond repair.

The girls, they'd been terrific. Phone calls. Fresh flowers sent to her classroom and here. Supportive e-mails, funny Hallmark cards. It helped. It all helped. Except...

Except that she'd loved him. Not the girlish dreamy love of her fantasies, but really honest-to-goodness love. She'd fallen for the man he was. Fallen hard. Ironic, huh? Be careful what you ask for. She'd heard that a hundred times and it had never meant anything to her. Now, she understood. She'd had her night. She should have been a lot more specific.

She got up, went back to her vegetables, to her brown rice. But she didn't finish it this time, either. Someone rang her doorbell.

She turned to Boo. ''You just keep eating. I'll get it.'' He flicked his tail in her general direction.

It was probably Hope. Or maybe Lily. Julia had come by last night, so she'd probably been given the evening off. The bell rang again.

''Hold on, darn it.'' She grabbed the knob and pulled open the door.

''Hi.''

Oh, God. ''Scott.''

He nodded.

She stared at him, at his pressed white shirt, his tan jacket, the gorgeous bouquet of flowers in his left arm and the two-pound box of chocolates in his right. What the heck—

''I was hoping I could come in. Just for a minute.''

She stepped back. As he walked by her, she

caught his scent in the air. A lump formed in her throat and her eyes burned threatening tears.

He stood in the living room, shifting on his feet, swallowing hard. As nervous as a sixteen-year-old on his first date. "These are for you," he said, holding out the flowers and candy.

"Thank you," she said, taking the flowers. "Although I'm not sure if I should thank you." She nodded at the candy. "Especially not for that."

"You don't like chocolate?"

"I love chocolate. Too much."

"I don't get you."

She studied his face, his eyes, trying to find the lie. But he genuinely seemed not to understand. She thought about telling him to skip it, but what was one more humiliation? "I'm working at losing weight."

His gaze immediately moved down her body. She wished like fire that she had worn one of her old dresses that hid most of her sins. His gaze was already moving back up until, finally, he reached her eyes. "Why?"

"Why what?"

"Why are you working on losing weight?"

"Come on, Scott. That's not necessary."

"What the hell are you talking about?" he said, his voice impatient and a little gruff. "All I'm saying is that I think you look great. You've always looked great."

"I—" She bit off her denial. The way he looked at her, she could almost believe he meant it. Which made no sense. "I thought you went more for girls like Cathy."

"You think that's why I was with her? Because she's skinny?"

"Partly."

"What I told you before was the truth. Emily, I don't care about her weight or your weight or my weight. It has nothing to do with it."

"It has nothing to do with what?"

"Whether a person is someone I respect. Someone I care about. But I can take these back. Hell, if it would make you happy, I'll throw them down the disposal."

"No. You don't have to do that."

He exhaled and as he did so, his mouth softened into a gentle smile and his eyes looked at her in a completely different way. "Hey. You're talking to me."

"Oh. Yeah. I guess I am." She wanted it to sound casual, but the truth was the second he said that she went quietly nuts. Her head told her to kick the bum out, but her heart, oh, her heart argued for mercy, and not for him. The ache was gone. Vanished. Although she could feel some other things, like her pulse beating double time, her cheeks flush, and much to her chagrin, she felt the need to squeeze her legs together. All her sober talk of just a little while ago was just so much blather now. Now that he had come to her.

She still wasn't sure what to make of his comments. Of course, he couldn't mean it. Not the way she wanted him to. But still, it felt good. Really good.

"I'm sorry," he said.

"For what?"

"For getting drunk. For being a jerk."

"I haven't forgiven you."

"So the flowers and the candy didn't work, eh?"

She smelled the gorgeous bouquet. "They worked a little."

"That's something, at least."

She grinned. "I'd better put these in water."

He followed her into the kitchen, and she'd never been more aware of her butt. The blouse she had on was tucked into her pants. But she didn't hear gagging behind her, so he must not think she was *too* bad.

Boo meowed a welcome as he sat in the middle of the kitchen floor, then went back to grooming himself. She got a vase from the cupboard over the stove. Scott leaned against the fridge, watching her as she attended to the flowers.

"I wanted to tell you something," he began tentatively.

"What?"

"About some advice you gave me. About Cathy."

The vase nearly slipped out of her hands. She couldn't breathe, couldn't move. *Why* did she let him get to her like this?

"I broke it off with her. You were right."

She breathed. "I was?" *Then why did you call me Cathy?*

"I don't remember much about that night, and she didn't, either. But we talked it over today. It's for the best."

She whirled around, spraying the kitchen with water from her wet hands. "You broke up with her last Saturday?"

He nodded.

"Last Saturday at the Long Horn?"

His forehead furrowed. "Yeah. Why?"

"No reason." She turned around again, her mind going over the details of that night. He had to have known they were about to make love. Right? Drunk is one thing, but he had his fingers…she'd never been that drunk. She didn't know anyone who'd been that drunk. Maybe…

"But that's not the only thing I wanted to tell you."

She didn't turn. Not yet. She filled the vase, put it on the counter, then put the flowers in. The gerbera daisies were gorgeous, and so were the mums. In fact, the whole arrangement was perfect. Grabbing the dish towel from the cabinet door, she dried her hands. Only then did she turn to face him. "Shoot."

He looked at her for a long moment, then his gaze went down to Boo's food dish. "I've been thinking…"

"Uh-oh."

"About a lot of things."

"Like?"

"Like finding someone to replace me at the store. Someone my mother can count on."

"Oh."

"My agent called again yesterday to tell me the ESPN job is still open."

"Do you think your mother will be okay?"

"I don't know. I hope so. The thing is, I need to talk to you about this. About everything."

"You do?"

He nodded as he walked slowly toward her. "This trip home has had some surprises for me. The kids at the store, that's been great. Greater than I ever would have guessed."

"That's nice," she said, hardly aware she was even speaking. Scott had caught her gaze, and he didn't waver. Not even when he stood right in front of her.

"That's not the nicest surprise."

"It's not?"

He shook his head, still not letting go of her gaze.

"What is?"

He smiled. Touched her cheek with the back of his hand. "You."

She closed her eyes, not daring to move a muscle, not even daring to hope.

"Funny thing," he whispered. "I didn't get it until just now."

"Didn't get what?"

"That you're the reason I've been so crazy for the past couple of weeks. But I don't want to ruin things."

"You won't."

"Even if I do this?" He leaned forward that last little bit. She felt his sweet breath against her mouth. More afraid than she'd ever been in her life, she closed her eyes. If he stopped now…

He kissed her.

Chapter Thirteen

It took her completely by surprise. She'd expected him to pull back, to... *Oh heavens.* His lips, warm, urgent, on hers. His arms suddenly wrapped around her, holding her tight. His tongue seeking entry, teasing her to open her mouth.

All coherent thoughts vanished like vapor in the wind. Emily abandoned herself to her feelings. This was bliss. It was what she'd wanted forever. This kiss, this heat, this wanting between them. It was nothing like the other night. Because this time, he wasn't drunk. And he knew exactly who was in his arms.

His hands moved down her back to her waist, then up again, all the while his mouth worked magic. She tasted spearmint, a hint of coffee and something entirely unique. *Him.* Her arms went around his neck and before she even knew what she was doing, she pressed her body against his, crushing her breasts on his chest.

He moaned as he made love to her mouth, kissing her with such hunger she trembled in his arms. This was it. *This* was the night she'd prayed for. The night that would carry her through the rest of her life. Because as much as she hungered for him, as incredible as it was to know he wanted her, she didn't dare believe he was here to stay. He wasn't hers.

Scott pulled back from the kiss to look into Emily's eyes. To make sure he wasn't pressing too hard, too fast. To make sure she wanted him. Her lips were parted, moist, swollen with desire. Her eyes had become dark with passion. Her skin, so beautiful and soft, glowed slightly with heat. Although he couldn't see the rest of her, he felt her nipples, hard yet supple against his chest.

He wanted her. Wanted her more than he'd ever wanted Cathy. More than he'd wanted any woman. *Emily.* Emily, with her kind eyes, with her beautiful smile. Right in front of his nose all these years, and he'd never seen it.

He leaned forward, nipping her lower lip with his teeth as he breathed in her heavenly scent. What he wanted was friction. Friction and release. He wanted to be inside her, deep in that velvet heat. He wanted to see her lush body, the curves he felt beneath his hands.

Instead, he kissed her, harder this time, hard enough to make her whimper. The sound, the vibration from her mouth to his so intimate and erotic he grew painfully hard.

He pulled back a moment, trying to think clearly. He wanted to take her to bed, to make love to her. But it was all so new. She might not want to. She might throw him out on his ear.

"What?"

"I want…"

She smiled. "Do you?"

He nodded. Opened his mouth, but she put her fingers on his lips. "Do you want to make love with me?"

He nodded again.

"With me. Emily."

"With you. Only with you."

She sighed. "That's wonderful. Because I want to make love with you."

He took her hand away as his eyes grew serious. "I don't know, Emily. I don't know how long I'm going to be here. Hell, I'm not sure about anything."

She cleared her throat and stepped back. If he wasn't sure, she'd bow out. She'd make it her fault. Because she knew with everything in her that she couldn't pretend anymore. She wanted him wanting her. All the way.

He pulled her back close. "Let me rephrase that. I'm not sure about my career. I'm very sure about what I want to do. The thing is, I can't give you any promises.''

''I'm not asking for any.''

''It's more complicated than that.''

''There's nothing complicated about what I want to do right now. In fact, I've heard it comes quite naturally.''

He chuckled, and she felt his body vibrate. ''Naturally, huh?''

She nodded.

''So you wouldn't mind if I do this—'' His hand moved down to the junction of her thighs, to the moist heat that had been building since he walked in the door.

She wriggled as his wicked fingers did their worst. ''Not at all.''

''Okay then. I think we're ready for the next step.''

''And what would that be?''

His move was so smooth, so sure, it was as if he'd rehearsed it a hundred times. He lifted her in his arms. Her! And he carried her through the kitchen, through the living room, all the way to her bedroom. And when he got there, he didn't put her down right away. Instead he kissed her.

She couldn't believe it. She'd been carried to her bed by Scott. Her Scott. The one man in all the world that could turn her to mush with a look.

He put her down carefully so her head was on

her pillow. The way he looked at her made her feel like Marilyn Monroe.

Scott took a moment. He was too close to the edge for comfort and he needed to cool his jets. He smiled at Emily, so incredible right there, waiting for him. Then he forced his gaze up.

The decor was everything he expected her bedroom to be. Lush and romantic, like something from a movie. Her four-poster was white, with a preponderance of pillows and thick with a feather bed. A full-length mirror made of the same dark wood as the bed frame dominated one corner, and a matching armoire the other. The only picture on the wall was of a naked woman sprawled seductively on a chaise. The colors were as vivid and beautiful as Emily herself.

Emily touched his leg. His gaze went to hers once more. "Now what?" she asked.

"Now I teach you. And you teach me."

She nodded as she sat up. Her hands went to the buttons of her blouse and a moment later it was on the floor. He stopped her as her hands went back to unhook her bra.

"Not so fast," he said. "I want you to undress for me. Slowly."

She let her hands drop as pink tinged her cheeks. Her gaze shied away, but only for a moment. Scott sat on the bed, sinking into its pillowy depth.

"I don't know if I can," she said.

"If you don't want to, it's okay. I understand."

She closed her eyes for a moment, then looked at him again. He wanted to see her naked. More than that, he wanted her to undress in front of him. Whenever she'd pictured this moment, it had been in the dark. She could see him, but in her dreams, she was hidden.

This was no dream. It was her one night. The night of her life. No way she was going to let fear get in the way. Her hands went to her slacks and she hooked the waistband in her fingers and pushed the material down, taking her time, moving her hips sensually from side to side. When her pants got past her hips, she let them drop.

Scott felt his heart slam against his ribs as he looked at her exquisite body. Her bra and panties were both red satin. The contrast between the material and her pale skin delighted him further, and he knew he would have to do something about it soon.

He held back though, mesmerized as Emily ran her fingertips up her tummy, up her chest. Her fingers found her nipples and circled them just once.

He took a deep breath, then let it out slowly as he took off his shirt and tossed it on the floor. His shoes and socks came next, all the while his gaze never wavered. And as he watched, he became more and more uncomfortable. He needed to be inside her, he needed release. It was no use. He cŏuldn't stand it. There was no way he could sit still for another second. "Wait."

She stopped and he got off the bed and approached her. He kissed her lightly on the lips, then took her hand and led her to the other side of the bed, to the mirror.

He stepped behind her, so she could see her reflection, and his at the same time. He kissed her neck, then ran his fingertips over her tummy, her chest, circling her nipples, so hard beneath the shimmery satin.

She leaned back against his bare chest, her gaze on his movements as he learned her body. He traced the outline of the bra, then let his fingers sneak inside the material. Her flesh felt twice as luxurious as the satin, so smooth it made him shake. "Can you see how beautiful you are?" he whispered. "This," he said as he ran his hands down her sides, luxuriating in the womanly curves. "So soft. So incredibly sexy."

He ached in earnest now, but he didn't want to hurry. He also didn't want to embarrass himself before they were even in bed.

She grabbed his pant legs to steady herself, and he noticed her chest rise and fall rapidly. He wasn't the only impatient one. Bowing to her wishes, he moved his hands to the clasp of her bra, and a second later, it was unhooked. "Take it off for me," he whispered.

As her hands went to her bra straps, his palms went down her tummy, over the slight, womanly swell. His left hand was content to stay there, to relish the feel of her skin. But his right hand couldn't leave well enough alone. His fingers traveled down, under the waistband of her panties, then farther, through the soft curls, lingering there for a moment.

Emily exhaled a deep breath, then removed her bra, leaving her breasts bare to both of them.

She was exquisite. Perfect. Full and round with her hard, long nipples. He moved his hips, pressing against her. "See what you do to me?"

His hand shifted in her panties. Parting her lips, his finger moved unerringly to the swollen bud at the very center of her pleasure. He circled it, eliciting a moan. He smiled in anticipation of what came next.

He stopped circling her and honed in, very gently, until he had her just where he wanted her. Then, as her eyes widened with surprise, he started moving his finger very quickly, like a master violinist on a perfect chord.

Emily gasped and gripped his legs desperately. A few seconds later, just as he felt her whole body tighten like the strings of a bow, he stopped. She cried out. But he didn't keep her waiting long. Moving in front of her, his back to the mirror, he went to his knees, pulling her panties down and then off, tossing them to the floor.

Breathing deeply the scent that aroused him nearly to the breaking point, he used his fingers to part her lips. He leaned forward that last inch and tasted her for the first time. He'd never been more anxious yet more determined to take it slowly. He wanted her to remember this night forever.

He closed his eyes as he pleasured her, until she gripped his hair tightly with both hands, until she quivered, until she cried out over and over.

Her head lolled back when he stopped, but her body kept trembling even as he stood, lifted her in his arms and carried her to the bed.

Before she had a chance to recover, he stripped off his pants, groaning as the air hit his erection.

"Oh, my."

He looked at Emily, who was staring at him. Her hand reached out and she touched him, very tentatively. He gritted his teeth, the combination of straining pain and intense pleasure almost too much to bear.

"You're wonderful," she whispered.

He laughed, but even that didn't ease the tension in his body.

"No, I mean it. You're gorgeous."

"You are."

She smiled. Closed her eyes. And as he watched, a single tear ran down her cheek.

"Em? Are you okay? We can stop now, if you want."

"No. No. I want you. I want this. Oh, I want to do everything."

"Everything?"

She nodded.

"I think that's a very worthy goal." He inched up the bed, maneuvering himself between her legs.

"Wait," she said. "In that drawer."

He looked to where she was pointing, then leaned over, nearly breaking his leg. But he got the drawer open and saw the small box of condoms. He grinned as he shook out the box and grabbed a silver packet. "I like a woman who's prepared."

"I'm a regular Boy Scout."

She laughed as he straightened up and took care of business.

"I don't think we're going to earn all our merit badges right now."

"No?"

He shook his head. "So why don't we concentrate on doing one thing very, very well."

Emily smiled wickedly. "One thing, eh?"

He nodded, moving up farther, running his hands under her legs and when he got to her knees, he lifted them, and pushed them back as he got closer and closer.

"So what would that one thing be?" she asked.

"I'll let you choose." He saw that her hands

had gone to her breasts. That she was rubbing her nipples as she watched him, and he wondered if she even realized what she was doing. His gaze flickered between her eyes and her fingers, not sure which view gave him more pleasure.

"Okay," she said, her voice teasing. "I think that one thing should be kissing."

"Sorry, ma'am. That's an incorrect answer." He'd moved as far as he needed to go. He was inches away from her, so close he could feel her heat. Her legs were still in his arms, pushed back so he could see her fully. So he could admire her totally.

"Incorrect?" Her voice had gone all feathery as her breathing went into high gear.

"I guess I'll have to show you."

She nodded. And then she lifted her hips off the bed. Just an inch or so. It was enough. Nothing on earth could have stopped him from sinking into her.

Emily felt him inside her, moving slowly, his thickness filling her inch by inch. It was an incredible, indescribable feeling, as if she'd been empty her whole life waiting for this man, for this moment.

He leaned forward, his gaze electrified, reflecting exactly the heat burning inside her. Then he moved again, filling her more deeply. She was able to put her arms around his neck, and pull him to her lips.

As they kissed, he thrust in farther, stopping when she gasped.

"Emily? Are you...?"

She nodded. "The last one in North America, I think."

He groaned as he pulled out.

"What are you doing?"

"Making sure you know what *you're* doing."

"I want nothing more in this world than to make love with you," she whispered. "You're the one I wanted to share this moment with."

"Me?"

"Yes. You."

"Why didn't you tell me?"

She laughed. Shook her head. "It's not exactly the kind of thing I could announce over coffee."

"Damn it, Em. I feel like I've been cheated."

"So what are you waiting for?"

He kissed her again, long and hard. He eased into her again, and then with one sharp thrust he was in her fully. He grew still, his gaze anxious now, waiting for some sign that she was okay.

It took her a couple of moments to adjust. For the pain to ease away. When it did, she moved her hips, testing. To his credit, Scott let her call the shots. He stayed completely still as she grew bolder.

Finally the pain was completely gone and she'd moved back into the pleasure zone. She nodded, and his head dropped in relief.

He moved in her slowly, a rhythm designed to make her crazy. But the more her hips lifted to meet his thrusts, the quicker his movements became. His expression changed. The loving mien of a moment ago shifted into a look so intense, so focused on her that she felt they were the only two people in the universe.

He pumped into her, his strokes going ever deeper, building and building, until she trembled all over. He shifted position so each thrust rubbed her in the exact right spot, the friction, the heat, sending her to a place she'd never been before. She cried out over and over, the whole bed shook, Scott kissed her desperately and then she went over the edge, into an ocean of pleasure and release. Seconds later, he cried out, stiffened and as she squeezed him one more time, he joined her.

"Oh, Scott," she whispered, as he sort of collapsed on top of her. It wasn't uncomfortable. In fact, she rather liked it. Her hands explored his body as she continued to have tiny little quakes. His skin was damp with sweat, and that was sexy as hell.

"What have you done to me, Emily?"

"I don't know. What have I done?"

He lifted his head for a moment. "You nearly

killed me.'' His head fell back again, resting on the pillow beside her. Right near her ear, it turned out, as she discovered a second later. She shivered as he teased her there with his tongue.

''Scott?''

''Huh?''

''I never guessed it would be so different.''

''Different than what?''

She turned her head a little, embarrassed that she'd started the conversation.

''Come on, Em. Spill. Different than what?''

''Different than when I…you know. When I do it…myself.''

He groaned and she felt him twitch inside her.

''Hey.'' She pinched his butt. ''It's a perfectly natural thing for a woman to do.''

''I know. I know. It's just that—''

''What?''

He lifted his head again. ''You wouldn't understand unless you were a guy.''

''I doubt that, but I feel too delicious to argue.''

''Good. Hey, Emily?''

''Yes?''

''Just exactly how long have you been wanting to do this with me?''

''Since I was sixteen.''

''Are you kidding?''

She shook her head.

''Why didn't you tell me?''

"You wouldn't understand unless you were a girl."

"Cute. Very cute."

He nipped her ear, and she yelped. Then she just lay there, so intimately entwined with him that together they were a new being, not just him and her, but Them. Something entirely unique in all the world.

After a few moments, Scott groaned again.

"What now?"

"I have to move. I don't want to move, but I have to move."

"Poor baby."

He rolled over, and she felt an immediate chill. As if he'd anticipated that, he pulled the comforter from his side of the bed and covered her. Then he dashed to the bathroom. She took advantage of the situation and looked at his butt as he went. He was as perfect as a man could be. So beautiful it made her ache.

She thought about what he'd done. How he'd taken her to the mirror and let her see her own body through his eyes. For the first time in years, maybe ever, she'd liked what she saw. Even though she wasn't thin, it was all right. She was pretty. And she was pretty sexy.

He came back a few moments later and climbed under the covers. He snuggled up against her, his arm across her chest, his leg over her legs.

Emily's eyes fluttered closed as an extraordinary peace settled over her. She finally understood what all the fuss was about. Why the poets spent so much time rhapsodizing about love. Although, with a twinge, she remembered that though they'd *made* love, they weren't *in* love. At least, he wasn't. The fact didn't change how she felt. Warm, comfortable and complete. Scott had been worth waiting for, and she couldn't imagine having her first time be with anyone else.

No matter what happened, she would remember this night happily. Oh, she had no doubt that losing Scott would be torture, but it would be worse if they'd never shared this. It was the right thing for her. Because she was in love with him. Deeply, passionately, madly in love.

Chapter Fourteen

What the hell had happened? Scott looked at Emily with wonder and confusion. Emily had wanted this since high school? How was it possible he hadn't known that? She'd been his friend. His good friend. Of course he'd thought about making love with her, that was only natural. But he'd never considered that she'd want to make love with him.

The problem now became—what next? If it were up to him, he'd just kick back and wait to see what happened. But he knew Emily wouldn't be satisfied with that. She was a planner, the person who coordinated the picnics and the school projects. So what was he going to tell her?

That he was grateful that she was speaking to him again? That making love with her had shocked the hell out of him? That it was the most intense, the most satisfying sex of his life? That he wanted more, and yet he wasn't willing to give up the ESPN job?

Complications fell on top of each other in his head only to become silenced as he noticed she had fallen asleep. She looked incredibly peaceful and beautiful. Watching her aroused him again, stirred him in a way no other woman had before. He wanted to please her. To protect her.

What a mess. Between his family obligations, his career and now this, he didn't know if he was coming or going. He needed to talk to someone. He smiled. The person he needed to talk to was sleeping beside him. His best friend.

"I DON'T KNOW," Scott said. "The thing that scares me is hiring someone else, leaving, and then Mom getting sick."

Emily shifted a tiny bit so his leg bent more comfortably over her legs. She was nestled beside him, their heads resting on the same pillow, their bodies touching wherever they could. She was playing with the soft hairs on his chest, idly twirling them or letting them tickle her palm. Scott had opened up more completely than ever before. He'd come to her for advice. She was positive the last thing in the world he'd considered was that they would end up like this.

He absently rubbed her back, not realizing, she felt sure, that his casual touch thrilled her. Over and over, she kept mentally pinching herself to make sure this was real.

"But I've been thinking," he went on. "The guys from the team are turning out to be good employees."

"I'm not surprised. They want to impress you."

"It's not just about me. I think Coach has told them how important it is to be professional and to have pride in the work. I was looking at the schedule yesterday and we've got almost all after-school hours covered, except during practice and games. And Mom is thrilled. She loves coming to the store and talking to the boys. I think it reminds her of when I was that age."

"I imagine you're right. They're good kids. And you're right about them taking pride in their work. I can see it in their studies. In fact, I think working at the store should be part of their studies. Like a lab."

"Hmm," he said. He looked so adorable when he was thinking. She kissed him on the chin. Mostly because she could. He smiled and kissed her back, but not on the chin. He kissed her until her toes curled, but after a few minutes she pulled back. One more second and they would have had to postpone the discussion for quite some time.

He laughed, shaking his head.

"What?"

"You. Me. Us. Who would have thought?"

"Not me. Not like this."

"What are your friends going to say?"

She grinned. "Hallelujah."

"Really? You mean Hope isn't going to threaten me with bodily harm?"

"Oh, no. Hope and the others, they just want me to be happy."

"Are you?"

She nodded. "Yes."

"No regrets?"

"Not a one."

His brows furrowed as he studied her face. "I wish I knew what was going to happen."

"I do, too. I'd buy a lottery ticket."

"Ha-ha."

"You said it yourself. I'm cute."

"I'm serious, Em."

"Well, knock it off. The best thing will happen. Even if you can't see what the best thing is yet. Just trust that."

"How do you know?"

"Because you're here."

He didn't say anything for a long time. He just looked into her eyes. Never before had she felt so complete. So utterly content.

"They really like you."

"Who?"

"The guys at the store. I hear them talk about you sometimes."

"What do they say?"

"They think you're funny and smart, and they like your classes."

"You lie."

He made an *X* over his heart. "I'm telling the truth, the whole truth and nothing but the truth."

"Then, thank you."

"You're welcome."

"I still say you'd make a great teacher."

"That's what I was thinking."

She laughed at his audacity.

"No, not that. Coach has asked me to come by practice. To give him a hand with the varsity team."

"That's terrific."

He nodded. "I didn't realize... I didn't know I'd find things here."

"Are you trying to say that you're happy?"

"Yeah. I am. But—"

"Nope. That's all that matters. Everything else is somewhere out there. In tomorrow. In this bed, we're happy."

"In this bed, at least one of us is also hungry."

"Hmm. I've got some cold cuts. Bread. I can make a sandwich."

"*We* can make a sandwich." He sat up and she fought the urge to pull him back down. He got out of the bed, pulled on his jeans then put his hands on his hips. "Are you coming?"

"I'm right behind you."

THE PHONE INTERRUPTED snack time. They were back in bed and on a big tray between them was a loaf of bread, some low-fat roast beef and cheese and condiments ranging from mustard to pickles.

"That's Hope." Scott said, reaching for the can of diet root beer.

"Or Lily."

"Or Julia."

"Or Sam."

He grinned. "Or Zoey."

She nodded as the phone rang for the fourth time.

"Are you going to answer it?"

"Nope."

"Won't they be worried?"

"Yep."

"That's not nice."

"Oh, all right." She leaned across the bed slowly, hoping the ringing would stop before she got to the phone. It didn't. "Hello?"

"What happened?" Hope asked.

"I'll tell you later."

"What? Are you crazy?"

"No. Just busy."

"With Scott?"

"Yes."

"Busy how?"

"None of your business."

"Oh, my God! This is it, isn't it? Your night!"

Emily sighed. "Yes."

A screech that could have been heard in Oklahoma pierced her ear. Scott heard it too, and he got a little pink in the cheeks. "I'll talk to you later, Hope."

"No. Wait. Don't hang up. I need details. Specifi—"

Emily put the phone back on the charger. Then she turned off the ring. If anyone else called, and she was positive they would, she wouldn't hear it. Her machine would take the messages.

"You gonna eat that pickle?"

She looked down at her plate. She still had a quarter of a sandwich left, and the last sweet pickle. She loved sweet pickles. "Nope. You can have it."

He plucked it off her plate and instead of feeling cranky, she felt wonderful. He could have all her pickles.

She giggled.

"What?"

"Nothing. Nothing at all."

"You know what we need?" he asked. "A shower."

"Go ahead. There are fresh towels in the cupboard."

"No. You didn't listen carefully, Teach. *We* need a shower."

"Together?"

He nodded. "You wash my back…"

"The heck with that. If we're going to shower together the last thing I care about is my back."

He laughed as he got up, taking the tray over to her dresser. "You are cute," he said. "No denying it."

She sighed. "I know. I'm just damned adorable."

HE DIDN'T WANT TO GO. He had to go, but the urge to stay made him come up with a whole slew of justifications for not showing up at work. The only thing that kept him from playing hooky was the very real likelihood that his mother would step in for him.

Emily leaned against her front door, her arms wrapped around her waist, molding her robe against her body. He liked that he knew what was under there. That he'd touched and tasted all the juicy parts. His body reacted to his thoughts, making his pants uncomfortably tight. If he didn't leave soon, he wasn't going to leave at all. "I'll call you later," he said, forcing himself to sound calm.

"Okay. I'll be here. Except when I'm at the gym. And the grocery store."

"When will that be?"

She shrugged as she smiled. "I don't know. I just might spend the rest of the day in bed."

He winced. "That was hitting below the belt."

"Hmm. Then I must be doing it wrong. I never wanted to hit."

"Emily, what am I going to do with you?"

"With me? Nothing. Not right now. You have work."

"Right." He stepped back from the door. "Yes, I have to work."

"Go."

"I'm going."

"So?"

"I am! In a second." He rushed forward, pulled her into his arms and gave her another goodbye kiss. She was the one to step back. He would have held her forever.

"Scott. Work. Now."

He saluted her, turned around and headed for the stairs. Walking was no picnic, what with his pants so snug. He *had* to stop thinking about her.

He dug his keys out of his pocket as he got to his car. The crises seemed to be over. He doubted he'd be arrested for indecency. But not thinking about Emily, about the night, was proving to be a harder task.

Not to say there wasn't something just at the edge of his mind. He couldn't quite remember what it was, only that it was important. He turned the key, the engine roared to life, and he remembered.

Emily had talked about the guys. About a lab.

The idea blossomed even as he backed out of the parking space and by the time he reached the corner, he had most of the details worked out too.

Emily was brilliant! Now, if he could convince the school...

EMILY STARED at her phone machine. Since Hope's call last night, her machine had recorded eight more messages. She was pretty certain who'd called. And called again. She didn't blame them. Of course they were excited. They were part of this whole thing, weren't they?

The Girlfriends would have a lot to crow about. That's why she wouldn't tell them everything. Because she loved them too much, and they deserved to believe everything would work out perfectly. Later on, when Scott was gone for good, they'd get it. They didn't need to worry about that now.

Only she knew she was never going to make love with Scott again. That he would be leaving sooner than he expected. That he would be able to take that fabulous job at ESPN.

She knew, because she'd given him his answer. She'd told him how he could leave without hurting his mother or the store. The answer had been right in front of him. The kids from school. There was no doubt they could do the work, as long as they had a manager there. Someone who was already at the store would be ideal. Emily knew his mother.

She'd be pleased with the plan, even though she would miss Scott. It was much more important that Scott seize this opportunity.

Isn't that why she'd planted the idea? So he would fulfill his potential? So he wouldn't have a life filled with regrets?

She sank down on the couch. Boo jumped up and rubbed the back of her hand and she pulled him onto her lap for a pet. It hadn't occurred to her that in giving Scott his escape, she'd condemned herself to the very thing she was saving him from. She was the one who would have the regrets.

Before, she'd thought having one night would be enough. Now she understood she'd been a total fool. One night, last night, had been the introduction to a brand-new life. One she'd be haunted by forever. Because she couldn't stay there. In fact, it was already gone.

She sighed. There was nothing to do but get on with her life. A saying popped into her head that seemed especially appropriate now. *God, grant me the serenity to accept the things I cannot change, the courage to change the things I can, and the wisdom to know the difference.*

The prayer made her feel slightly better. But the road ahead of her was rocky with things she couldn't change, and she'd need all the serenity she could find. As for wisdom? The one thing she knew for sure, beyond all reason, was that the best thing would happen. It always did, as long as she was willing to see it.

Chapter Fifteen

Scott brought his mother her cup of tea then sat across from her at the dining room table. She looked good, better than she had when he'd arrived in Sheridan. With her hair done, wearing a pretty dress, she was like her old self again. It did him good to see her eyes light up when she smiled. That was the surest sign that her depression over his father's death was lifting.

"Bobby is ready to be a cashier, don't you think?" she asked.

He smiled gratefully. It was a perfect introduction to his talk with his mom. "Yes, I do. I think he's been a model employee."

"I get such a kick out of those boys. They're so kind. They carry my groceries, they fill up my car with gasoline, Bill Tobin was here all day Saturday weeding the garden."

"I'm glad you like them, Mom, because I have a proposition for you."

She nodded. "Let's hear it then."

"It was Emily's idea. She thought we could hire kids from the school to work at the store as sort of a class project. They'd learn all the different jobs, and by the end of the year, they'd have work experience under their belts, they'd have some extra money, and we'd have plenty of great help."

His mother sipped some tea. When she put her cup down, her gaze went to his and she looked at him the way she had all his life. Her intuition about him was uncanny, and he'd always felt she could look right through him. "I like it. It will give you the chance to take that job in Connecticut."

"I won't go if it doesn't work perfectly," he said, not at all surprised that she'd gone directly to the heart of the matter. "I'd like to make Miguel the manager. He knows as much about the store as I do. And there will be a faculty advisor, too."

"What about summertime?"

"You don't have to worry about that. The kids will sign up all year. They won't be in the store during school, but there are ways we can work that out. We'll need two full-time employees to rotate during the days. But we'll leave all the stocking and pricing for the kids. Mom, I think it'll work."

"What about the school? What do they have to say?"

"The principal is all for it. You know him, right? David Warren?"

She nodded. "He used to deliver the paper to the house."

"He did?"

"Oh, yes. He was a good boy."

Scott leaned forward and took her hand in his. It was so light, almost no weight at all, and her skin was nearly transparent. Maybe he shouldn't leave. Was the job so important?

"Scott, dear. I'm delighted. It's been weighing so heavily on me that you've had to come home—"

"I don't mind."

"Of course you don't. You're my angel. But I mind. My dearest wish is for you to have all you want out of life. I hope you get that job, and that it makes you happy. And I hope you find a nice girl and give me lots of grandchildren."

He grinned. "I'll work on it."

She squeezed his hand. "Just come to visit from time to time, will you?"

"You know I will."

Her smile let him know for sure that she was all right with the plan. He could hardly believe how things were falling into place. Two big pieces were missing, however. First, ESPN had to hire him. Second, Emily. What was he going to do about Emily?

THE PRINCIPAL LEANED BACK in his executive chair, rocking slightly as he considered Emily's suggestion. David Warren was a very tall man, six-five, and his chair barely fit him. He was an excellent principal, one who'd made her job a pleasure.

"I think it'll work," he said. "Except when you're working on the school play."

"Oh, right." She hadn't thought of that. "I can still be faculty advisor, but during the play, I'll get myself an assistant."

"It will have to be someone who won't charge us."

"I know, David. Believe me. I'll find someone. It'll work out."

"Great. Scott said it was mostly your idea."

"No. I just planted a small seed. He's the one that grew the plan."

"I think the kids are going to learn a lot from this. And if it works the way I think it will, perhaps other companies in the community will do the same thing."

"Right," she said. "It'll give the students an excellent start. Let them see what it's like to be in the real world. And how valuable a college education is."

David nodded. "I only wish we could have accommodated Scott's other idea. Although now it's a moot point. I hear he's going to Connecticut on Thursday."

Emily stiffened, struggling to keep her feelings to herself. To wear an easy smile. Inside, she was reeling. He was leaving on *Thursday?* It was too soon! What was it David had said? "What was his other idea?"

"He wanted to come on board as assistant coach. We'd have loved to have had him, but you know the budget. There's no way we could have afforded that."

"Of course not." She stood up, using every bit of strength she possessed to appear relaxed. "I've got a class in a few minutes. We'll talk again about the advisor position, okay?"

"Absolutely. And thank you, Emily."

"You're welcome." She left his office by the side door. Once she was in the hallway, she headed toward the exit. She had to leave, just for a few minutes, even though it meant she'd be late for class. The thing was, she couldn't face the students yet. The last thing she wanted to do was burst into tears in front of her kids.

She made it outside, then dashed across the lawn to the parking lot. She climbed into her car and slammed the door. Her eyes filled with tears as she laid her forehead on the steering wheel. What had she done? He had been prepared to stay, and she'd given him the perfect out. The only thing she hadn't done was pack his bags.

Why? Why hadn't she kept her mouth shut? She

had no interest in being a martyr. She wanted him to stay. So what if he gave up his dream? He'd find a new dream. One that included her.

She wiped her eyes. Sniffed. It wasn't fair. It wasn't fair to know heaven for only a moment. Because earth could never be the same again.

The tissue box was in the back seat. She plucked a half-dozen sheets, wiped her eyes, then pulled down the mirror on her visor. She looked like hell. Mascara was fine and dandy until it mixed with tears. It took her a few minutes to repair the damage. When her face looked somewhat normal again, she left her car and headed for class. No use postponing the inevitable. Some things were meant to be, even if it hurt like the very devil.

Scott needed his chance to fly. As for her? She'd get through it somehow. With the help of her Girlfriends.

HE DIDN'T BRING CANDY this time. Only his hat in his hand. The prospect of saying goodbye to Emily had eaten away at him all day. But the interview was on, the network was enthusiastic, and his manager had insisted the job was his.

She opened the door. Her smile nearly did him in. It was the saddest smile he'd ever seen. Brave and sad. ''Come on in.''

He stepped inside her apartment, wondering if

this was the last time. No. He'd come back to visit. He would.

"I hear you have great news."

He nodded. "News, but I'm not sure how great it is."

"Come on, Scott," she said, leading him to the kitchen. "Of course it's great. You deserve this chance. It's everything you ever wanted."

"I'm not so sure anymore."

"I'm sure." She wore a long dress, short sleeves, black with white designs. Her earrings were black and white, too, and once again he was struck by her beauty. It mystified him still that he'd taken her for granted for so long. How he'd never connected his feelings for her with action.

And now, it was too late. Ironic. Horribly ironic.

"Want something to drink?"

"Sure."

She busied herself getting glasses, ice and soda. He watched her and his thoughts turned to Connecticut. What would his life be like there? He knew no one, but that had never been a problem. He just wished the network wasn't so far away. He'd miss her. More than he could have ever guessed.

"Here," she said, handing him the glass. She sat down, and he took the seat beside her.

"I don't even know if I'm going to get the stupid job."

"You will. And you'll be wonderful."

"But…"

"But what? Scott, you don't have to worry about a thing. I'm going to be the faculty advisor to the kids at the store. I'll make sure it works."

"You are?"

"Didn't David tell you?"

"I haven't spoken to him since yesterday."

"It's a done deal."

"Em, you don't have to."

"I know. I want to."

"But what about…"

"The other night?" She smiled that same sad smile again. "It was perfect. And I'll always remember it. But, we both knew it wasn't going to last, right? We're friends. Buddies." She leaned forward and squeezed his hand. "I'm happy here. I love my job, my friends. My family is here. But you? Your destiny is somewhere else. In a much bigger world."

"How do you know?"

"I look at you and I know. You're on the threshold, Scott. Standing on the edge of an incredible life. You can't let anything distract you now. Especially not me."

"Why not you?"

She looked away for a long moment, and he wasn't sure what to do. But finally, her gaze came back to him, her eyes shimmering with unshed tears. "I have a confession to make."

"What's that?"

"I hope you'll take this the right way." She put her hands on her glass, squeezing it so tight he thought it might break. "I've had a crush on you for so long I can't even remember when it started."

Even though she'd told him the same thing last night, it was still a jolt to hear it.

"I'd dreamed of us being…intimate. My dreams were inadequate. It was so much nicer. But…"

"What?"

"Dear Scott. The thing is, it was a crush. A childhood crush carried on for too many years. I love you as a friend. Do you see?"

He sat back in his chair. Friends? That's all? He hadn't realized until this second that he'd assumed they were more. That she'd changed right along with him last night. He wasn't sure what it was between them, but it wasn't just friends.

"I don't get it. I thought—"

"I know. I thought so, too. But in the light of day it's clear to me that we weren't going to end up together. Even if you stayed here."

"Why not?"

She pressed her lips together tightly for a few seconds. Then she sighed. "Scott, I want to get married. I want children. And I want to do it with someone who likes it here as much as I do. I want a simple life. And that's something you can't give me.''

"We don't know that.''

"We do. You do.''

It was his turn to sigh. ''So, is that it? Is this goodbye?''

"Oh, it's not as dramatic as all that. We'll talk on the phone. You'll come to visit. I'll see you on television. Who knows? I might even start to like football.''

He smiled and he knew that his expression and hers were mirrors of each other. Sad, so sad. ''I'll miss you, Em.''

"I'll miss you, too.''

He stood up, held his hand out for her. She put her palm in his and stood beside him. He found her gaze and tried to memorize all the specks of gold in their brown depths. He kissed her gently on the mouth, memorizing her taste. Aching in a way he could hardly explain.

She turned away. Pulled her hand free. ''I hate to say it, but I've got papers to grade.''

"Okay.'' He knew she didn't. But he also knew it was time for him to leave. ''I'll let myself out.''

"Thanks!'' she said cheerfully, which made him feel ten times worse.

He hesitated. Wishing like hell he didn't have to go. Wishing she hadn't made it so easy for him. ''Goodbye, Em.''

She nodded, but she wouldn't meet his gaze.

"Em—"

"Go, Scott. Please."

He touched her arm with his fingertips. Then he walked out of the kitchen, out of the apartment, out of her life.

EMILY SANK INTO HER CHAIR. Tears flowed down her cheeks as she tried to remember how to breathe. Her lie felt heavy and sharp in her chest, like a wound that would never heal. She wanted to run after him, confess, beg him to stay. She wanted to tell him she loved him with all her heart and soul. That she would always love him.

Nothing had ever hurt this way. Nothing. It seemed impossible that she could live with pain like this. How could the clock keep ticking? The moon stay in the sky? How could she take even one more breath?

She'd gotten her wish. She'd had one night with Scott Dillon. Like something out of *Grimm's Fairy Tales,* she was now left with bitter regret. Be careful what you ask for. You might just get it.

She'd gotten it. Right between the eyes.

This was something The Girlfriends couldn't fix. No one could. It was a critical break, a fundamental shift. Nothing would ever be the same again.

"I THOUGHT YOU WERE LEAVING?"

Scott nodded. "Tomorrow."

"Well, come on in."

He walked past Hope, into her surprising living room. He sniffed an exotic scent, and he saw incense burning in a dragon's mouth. He sat down, wondering what he was going to say.

"What's going on?" she asked, curling up on the futon chair. Her outfit clashed with the decor. Old, worn jeans. A guy's white T-shirt. No shoes, no makeup. She looked so young. Just like she had in high school.

"I wondered if you'd talked to Emily."

She shook her head. "Only her answering machine. I went over there last night, but she wasn't there."

"Oh."

"Have you said your goodbyes?"

"Yeah. But..."

"What?"

"It didn't seem right. I can't stop thinking that I'm missing something."

"I'll give you credit, Scott, old boy. You may not be able to solve the puzzle, but you know when to ask to buy a vowel."

"Am I supposed to say thank you?"

"No. But after I tell you this, you'll want to."

He leaned forward. Almost afraid to hear what she had to say.

"Emily likes you," she said, but weirdly, the emphasis heavy on the second word.

"I know that. We talked about it. She used to have this crush and all, but after the other night, she just wants to be friends. And I respect that. I do. But something's wrong."

Hope nodded. "Some people would think she was lying about that. Not that I'm saying she was or anything."

"Lying? Why would she do that?"

"Pay attention. She *likes* you. She wants what's best for you."

He thought about that for several seconds, and then it dawned on him. "She wants to make it easy for me to leave."

"Three points and an extra spin on the wheel for you."

"What am I supposed to do?"

Her expression turned serious. "That's one you'll have to figure out for yourself. The reason she wanted you to go was so that you wouldn't have regrets. She didn't want you to resent her."

"I wouldn't."

"No?"

"Oh, man. I don't know. I honest to God don't know."

"I think you'd better go to Connecticut," Hope said. "I think the answers might come when you're gone."

"I don't want to hurt her."

"I know. And so does she."

"How come things get so complicated?"

She shrugged. "I don't know. Everything confuses me."

"You? I don't believe that."

She smiled. "Then my plan worked!"

"Hope, you are some piece of work."

"You're not so bad yourself. Oh. I wanted to tell you. I saw Cathy the other night."

He put his head in his hands and groaned.

"Don't worry. She's not devastated. I think her pride was hurt a little, but she's making an excellent recovery."

"What does that mean?"

"It means, she was out with Bud Fargo. And they looked pretty lovey-dovey, if you ask me."

"Bud Fargo. Yeah, sure. I remember him. He's a good guy."

"She seemed to think so."

"I'm glad."

"Yeah, I thought you would be."

"What about you, Hope? Is there someone in your life?"

"Alas, no. The last guy who asked me out was Phil Homes."

"Who?"

"You know him. I believe he's a guard on the varsity football team."

"*That* Phil Homes?"

"He thought I was in high school."

Scott stood. "Whoever finds you is going to be a very lucky man."

"You silver-tongued devil," she said as she rose to walk him to the door. "I hope things work out for you and Emily."

He leaned down and kissed her on the cheek. "You've been a good friend."

"I'll continue to be one. If you need me, call. I'll do my best. But remember, Emily comes first. Sorry, that's just the way things are."

"Thank goodness she has you."

"Yeah, yeah. They all say that."

He grinned, but he could see Hope's words were falsely cavalier. "I'll be in touch."

Hope closed the door behind him, but he didn't walk to his car just yet. If Hope was right, Emily loved him. It was tempting to believe that. But he couldn't. If it was true, he needed to hear it from Em. He needed to see her face when she said it.

The question was, did he love her? What was this thing that had happened to him, if not love?

This was why he liked football. Get the ball, throw the ball, find the goal line. Simple.

There was nothing simple about Emily. Not one blessed thing.

Chapter Sixteen

Emily pulled out her high school yearbooks and took them to the couch. Boo was already there, and he meowed his permission for her to sit down. Of course, there were conditions. She had to pet him a good long while before she could do anything else.

Finally Boo was satisfied, and she opened the first book. Tenth grade. What an awkward year that had been. She'd been a late bloomer, but when she finally sprouted it had been dramatic. For most of the year, she had walked around with her books held tightly to her chest, trying to hide the evidence of her maturity. None of the other Girlfriends had boobs as big as hers, not even Zoey.

Oh, gosh, there was Hope. The candid photo had been snapped on the quad, under the big tree. Hope had been in her military phase, wearing camouflage and a radically short hairdo. Even so, she looked years younger than she was.

Emily turned the page to find a photo she'd all but forgotten. The Girlfriends in all their glory. She, pudgy, timid, hiding behind Lily. Samantha, so beautiful and so unaware of it. Hope with her buzz cut, trying to look older. Zoey, her hair a wild mass of curls, her smile silver with her hated braces. Julia. Perfect Julia. Photogenic, slender, gorgeous but also sad. After all these years Emily still didn't know why. Of all of them, Julia was the most private. And of course the big ham Lily, arms spread wide, goofy smile, skirt so short it should have been outlawed.

Emily smiled, studying the faces on the page, this wonderful slice of her personal history. They'd done it. They'd stayed close all these years. She loved her friends as if they were her sisters. Sighing, she turned the page.

There he was, in a photo that filled half the page. Scott. Oh, he'd been stunning even back then. Particularly when he wore his football uniform with those fake shoulders. His helmet was under his arm, his smile confident, and his hair was long and wild. She'd dreamed of him this way for a whole year. Every night, she'd flipped to this picture just before going to sleep. The only thing that had replaced it was a similar picture in the eleventh-grade yearbook.

But that was then, this was now. Scott was gone, off to conquer new heights, win fresh accolades.

The last thing he'd be thinking about was the girl he'd known in high school. Sure, their night together had been spectacular, but Scott wasn't the type to dwell on the past. He had always looked forward, never back.

Which was just what she needed to do. She needed to see a future for herself, without Scott Dillon. Even though she couldn't imagine it right this second, she felt sure that in time she would. All she had to do was live until then. And stop thinking about him! Her gaze went down to his picture. *Yeah, right.*

SCOTT PACED IN HIS HOTEL ROOM from the window to the door and back again. Should he call her again? No. He should wait until he had some definitive news. He stopped mid-stride and went to the honor bar. Beer. Oh, no. Not that. He wasn't on speaking terms with booze of any kind. Macadamia nuts. Nope. Candy bar?

He slammed the little door shut, grabbed the remote control and turned on the TV. Of course, he turned to ESPN first. It was "SportsCenter." He sat on the bed and watched, but his concentration was nil. He thought about the interview tomorrow. His second in two days. This time, with the big guy. But even that couldn't hold his full attention. Emily had too strong a hold on him. She hadn't left him alone for ten minutes. Her voice was in his head. Her perfume was on every woman he passed. He kept thinking he saw her, at the airport, in a restaurant

What in hell was he going to do about Emily? It wasn't fair. He didn't need this now, not with so much at stake. But every time he tried to shut her out of his mind, she sneaked back in.

Something had happened between them. At least, something had happened to him. It wasn't like anything else he'd experienced before. Hope had hinted…oh, man. He was in trouble. Deep trouble.

Should he call her again?

THE WEEK INCHED BY and Emily somehow trudged through it. Despite the ache in her heart, she went to the gym four times. She ate salads and drank eight glasses of water a day. She exfoliated her skin, gave herself a pedicure, remembered her sunblock and she even called her mother twice. But with each passing day it seemed harder and harder to remember why she was being so vigilant.

Scott had phoned from his hotel in Connecticut, but it had been a short, awful conversation. He was nervous before his big interview and she didn't want him to know she was upset. There were these long pauses, which had never happened between them before. She was the one to say goodbye first. It wasn't a choice. If she'd stayed on any longer she would have fallen completely apart—the last thing she wanted to do to Scott the night before his big chance.

Lily, Hope and Julia had been incredible troupers. They'd rallied around her, offering soft shoulders to cry on, sympathetic ears and constant reinforcement that she was doing the right thing. Zoey and Sam had called every day to let her know they were thinking of her.

Despite all that, she had no desire to go tonight. A football game at the high school was the last thing she needed. Everything would remind her of what she'd lost. The crowd filled with couples. The terrible band. Even the hot dog vendor. What she wanted to do was stay home, crawl into bed with a variety of sinful treats, most especially some Ben & Jerry's Triple Chocolate Fudge, and watch old movies. That wasn't too much to ask for, right? One night?

Her eyes closed as she realized what she'd said. The last time she'd asked for one night, she'd gotten far more than she bargained for. God, how she missed him!

The store project had already launched with a planning session on Wednesday. Bobby Knight had taken on the task of teaching the new students the ropes. Emily had been surprised to find Gretchen Foley had signed up for the project. Gretchen didn't seem the type who would willingly bag groceries. But a lot of kids wanted in, boys and girls. Emily understood. In a town where the status quo doesn't even shake with a large breeze, anything new and different was eagerly sought after. The bragging rights of working in Scott Dillon's store would be enough to shift the social status of some of the less popular students.

But the meeting had been particularly hard for her. Every other word seemed to be "Scott." The gossip was that he had a model waiting for him in Connecticut. Sara Wilding from the store had reported that Scott had gotten a lot of calls from Hollywood, each one a female.

Emily had smiled through it all. Her facade hadn't cracked an inch. But she hadn't slept that night. Or last night, either. She was overtired and overwhelmed. What she wanted was to do nothing, to think nothing, and mostly to feel nothing.

The phone rang. Emily sighed as she picked up the receiver. "Yes, Lily," she said, cutting her friend off at the pass. "I'm getting dressed."

"Good. Because I'm leaving right now."

"Are you sure you wouldn't rather eat popcorn and watch *The Way We Were?*"

"I'm positive."

"Fine, have it your way."

"I always do," Lily said in that tone of hers.

"Ha."

Lily sniffed. "I know."

Her voice had changed. Weariness tinged her words, and Emily knew immediately that Lily's job and her son and life in general had conspired against her.

"Can't I at least pretend I can have my way sometimes?"

"Ah, Lily. Has it been one of those days?"

"Don't ask."

"I won't. I'll wait till I see you."

"Good. Now go change whatever you're wearing for something sexy."

Emily had to smile as she hung up the phone. In fact, she'd planned to wear an oversize sweatshirt and her baggy jeans. Her friends knew her too well, that's all. She'd have to do something about that. But not tonight. Tonight she needed every old comfort she could find.

SHE LOST INTEREST in the game about forty seconds after the coin toss. Her gaze traveled over the crowd as the Tigers struggled for a first down. She knew ninety percent of the kids on the bleachers. They'd either been in her class, or had siblings in her class, or they were the children of friends. She wondered what it would be like to live in a big city. To walk the streets anonymously, not worrying what the neighbors thought. Actually, she didn't care what the neighbors thought, at least most of the time. But she kept feeling that this time her private tragedy had gone public. Everyone was looking at her. But she never met anyone's eye. As soon as she turned, they looked away. It didn't happen two or three times, but ten, twenty times. Very, very weird.

"Lily?" She leaned to her right until her shoulder met Lily's.

"What?"

"Do I have to stay for the whole game?"

"Yes."

"Why?"

"Because I love football and you love me."

Emily kicked her purse, tipping it over. Her lipstick tumbled out and rolled under the seats. Sighing heavily, she knelt in front of her seat and bent to find the black tube. It had gone farther than she thought, two seats down. But, if she stretched...

Her hand went out, she shifted once, again, stretching her fingers as far as they would go. The man next to her lifted his feet. The woman next to him lifted her feet, too. And then a masculine arm came down and plucked the lipstick from the ground. Emily's gaze went to his boots, and something deep in her stomach clenched with an excitement so strong she nearly lost her balance. His legs, clad in worn Levi's, narrow and so tall she had to sit up to see his belt. His dark blue polo shirt held shoulders that could only belong to one man. It was then she realized everyone around her had grown quiet. The stillness made her more aware of the pounding of her heart.

His hand reached out and she took it, letting his strength pull her to her feet.

"Hey," he said, his voice low and intimate despite the crowd.

"Hey."

"Got a minute?"

She nodded. Or at least she thought she nodded. He leaned slightly to his left. "I'll bring her back."

"Don't hurry on my account," Lily said.

Then Scott pulled her along in back of him as they stepped over feet and soft drinks until they reached the stairs. She could hardly believe it was him, hardly believe he'd come back. He must not have gotten the job. She felt guilty as hell for the happiness inside her, the selfishness that made her never want to let go of his hand again.

They made it to the stadium floor. Scott squeezed her hand as he led her away from the field toward the school. Students stepped aside, clearing the way for them, smiling at her as if they shared her excitement and anticipation. He hurried once they reached the phys ed building, and she almost had to run after him to keep up.

Finally they got to the quad, the center between four buildings where she'd eaten lunch a hundred times, where she'd watched this man and dreamed a dream she could hardly believe might come true. He brought her to the oak tree, and waited for her to sit. Once she was perched on the concrete bench, he sat facing her.

"You've come back," she said, wanting to say so much more but not knowing how.

He nodded. "I have some news."

"Yes?"

His mouth curved into a satisfied grin. "I got it. I got the job."

Her heart stopped beating. Oh, God, what a fool she'd been to think— He wasn't here to tell her he loved her, he was here to say a last goodbye!

"But that's not all."

She smiled, although she had the feeling her expression was far more tragic than happy. She didn't want him to know he was killing her. It wasn't his fault. It was her own. The dream had turned to a nightmare, and—

"I turned it down."

Emily swallowed even though her mouth was as dry as the desert. "Excuse me? What did you say?"

"I turned the job down."

"Why?"

"I got a better offer."

He wasn't making any sense. Or maybe he was and it was she who couldn't make sense of the words. "At ESPN?"

"Nope."

"I...I'm...I..."

He laughed. He leaned forward took her shoulders in his hands and kissed her. Kissed her hard and long and she'd never felt anything better in her whole life. When he finally pulled back, his hand went to her cheek. He caught a tear with his thumb. She hadn't realized she was crying.

"I got another offer. I'm the new coach at Sheridan College."

"*Our* Sheridan College?"

"Yep. Thirty minutes from home, with traffic."

"But..."

"But," he said, his gentle eyes filled with tender humor. "But it will only be a better offer if you say yes."

"Yes to what?"

"What do you think?"

She blinked twice. Then again.

"I love you. I don't know why it took me so long to figure it out, but there you have it. I love you. I love this town. I want to teach, just like Coach taught me. But mostly I want to go to sleep with you every night. I want to wake up next to you every morning. I want to have children with you. Lots of them. I want to grow old with you by my side."

Emily tried to breathe, but the lump in her throat made that impossible. She touched his face with trembling fingers, made sure he was there in the flesh and that this wasn't a hallucination. His skin was warm. And when she leaned in to kiss him, his lips were soft and gentle.

"Are you going to keep me in suspense?" he whispered, his lips almost touching hers.

"I should," she said. "But I won't."

"So you'll marry me? You'll be my wife?"

"Yes. I'll marry you."

He shot up, bringing her with him. This time his kiss wasn't so gentle. It was hard and hot and filled with the promise of a thousand more just like it. His arms went around her waist and he lifted her up in the air, still kissing her, twirling her around in a circle.

He didn't need to use much strength. She was flying, soaring on her own. Scott Dillon loved her! And she loved him right back.

It was everything she'd ever hoped for. All she'd dreamed of. But…she pulled her head back. "Are you sure? Are you sure you want to give all that up?"

He put her down again, but held her captive with his gaze. "More sure than I've ever been about anything. I love coaching. Much more than I would ever enjoy being on TV. This way I can try to make a difference in people's lives."

"You'll be a wonderful coach."

"I want to be a wonderful husband." He

touched her under her chin. "I should have known years ago that this is what my life was meant to be."

"No. Now is the perfect time."

He nodded. "Perfect." Then he kissed her.

Epilogue

Five months later...

"Do you, Scott Dillon, take Emily Proctor to be your lawful bride? To have and to hold from this day forth, through sickness and health, forsaking all others?"

Emily held her breath as Scott said, "I do." The way he looked at her made her feel like the luckiest woman on earth.

"Do you, Emily Proctor, take Scott Dillon to be your lawful husband?"

"I do," she said, not even hearing the rest of the minister's words. She had always belonged to Scott. From the first day they'd met, all through school, and even when he'd gone on to college and the pros. She'd been his. And now, he was hers.

She glanced at her bridesmaids—Hope, Lily, Sam, Zoey and Julia, all in their soft pink gowns, all of them ruining their makeup with happy tears. The Girlfriends had done it. They'd banded together and helped her reach her finest moment. Was any woman luckier than Emily?

The thought brought her gaze back to the man she loved. As the minister said the final blessing, Scott smiled at her with more love than any person deserved.

"By the power invested in me by the state of Texas, I now pronounce you husband and wife. You may kiss the bride."

Scott leaned forward and she met him halfway. He kissed her, thrilling her down to her toes. This was it—the most perfect moment of her life.

He pulled away a scant inch, his lips still touching hers. "Thank you," he whispered.

"For what?"

"For loving me back."

HOPE SIPPED HER CHAMPAGNE as she eyed the gorgeous wedding cake. Emily and Scott, married for three whole hours already, were about to cut the first slice. Tears filled her eyes again. She tried to stop them. She'd done nothing but cry all day. But she couldn't help it. As she glanced at the other Girlfriends, she saw they couldn't help it, either. It was just so…perfect!

"I can't stand it," Lily whispered.

"I know," Hope said. "Can you believe we did it?"

Julia shook her head. "I wonder…"

"What?" Lily asked.

"If we could do it again."

Hope laughed. But not for long. Because Lily, Zoey, Sam and Julia had all turned to face her. "Hey, wait a minute…"

"You're the one who's been complaining about not having a man in your life," Zoey said.

"And how you can't find any decent men in Sheridan," Lily added.

"No." Hope put her glass down on the closest table. "No. And that's final. I'm not letting you nuts anywhere near my love life."

Zoey grinned. Lily smiled. Julia nodded.

"Relax," Sam said, taking a step toward her. "It won't hurt a bit. Just ask Emily."

They all turned toward the happy couple. The cake had been cut, a slice on the plate between them. Scott's hand was halfway to Emily's mouth. But somewhere between cutting the cake and feeding it to his new bride, he'd gotten lost in his lover's eyes.

Zoey sniffed. "If Hope doesn't want to be next, I do."

Julia shook her head. "No. Me."

"I should be next," Lily said. "I've got a son to think about."

"No," Sam said, "I'm the oldest. I think it should be me."

Hope turned to face her friends. "We'll decide the old-fashioned way. By catching the bouquet."

One by one, The Girlfriends nodded. And waited breathlessly for Emily to finish kissing Scott and put the plate down. Em headed for the staircase, her bouquet still in her hands. The girls followed, trying to keep a stately pace.

Finally Emily was on the fifth step up. She turned so her back was toward them. And then she threw the bouquet over her right shoulder.

Everyone dived for the flowers. But only one hand caught them....

* * * * *

Who's next on The Girlfriends' list?
Stay tuned for the next

GIRLFRIEND'S GUIDE

coming to you in 2001
only from Jo Leigh and
Harlequin American Romance!

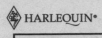

Tyler Brides

It happened one weekend...

Quinn and Molly Spencer are delighted to accept three
bookings for their newly opened B&B, Breakfast Inn Bed,
located in America's favorite hometown, Tyler, Wisconsin.

But Gina Santori is anything but thrilled to discover her
best friend has tricked her into sharing a room with
the man who broke her heart eight years ago....

And Delia Mayhew can hardly believe that she's
gotten herself locked in the Breakfast Inn Bed
basement with the sexiest man in America.

Then there's Rebecca Salter. She's turned up at the
Inn in her wedding gown. Minus her groom.

*Come home to Tyler for three delightful novellas
by three of your favorite authors: Kristine Rolofson,
Heather MacAllister and Jacqueline Diamond.*

HARLEQUIN®
Makes any time special ™

Arriving this December from

TWIN EXPECTATIONS
by
Kara Lennox

Identical twins Liz and Bridget Van Zandt always
dreamed of marrying and starting families at the
same time. But with their biological clocks ticking
loudly and no suitable husbands in sight, the
sisters decided it was time to take action.

Their new agenda: Have babies without
the benefit of grooms. They never expected
they'd meet two eligible bachelors whose
destinies were about to crash headlong
into their carefully laid plans....

**Don't miss the fun and excitement in this special
two-stories-in-one volume from Kara Lennox
and Harlequin AMERICAN *Romance*!**

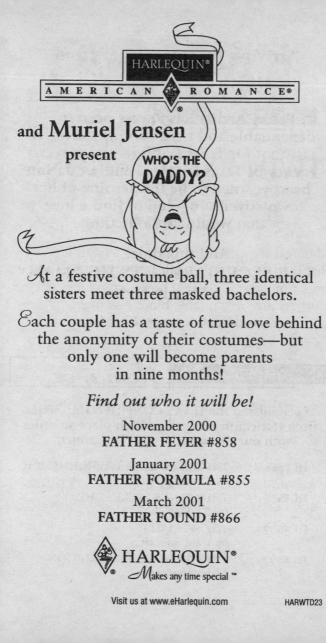

Penny Archer has always been the
dependable and hardworking executive
assistant for Texas Confidential, a secret
agency of Texas lawmen. But her daring
heart yearned to be the heroine of her
own adventure—and to find a love
that would last a lifetime.

And this time...
THE SECRETARY GETS HER MAN
by Mindy Neff

Coming in January 2001 from

HARLEQUIN®

AMERICAN *Romance*

If you missed the TEXAS CONFIDENTIAL series
from Harlequin Intrigue, you can place an order
with our Customer Service Department.

HI #581	THE BODYGUARD'S ASSIGNMENT by Amanda Stevens
HI #585	THE AGENT'S SECRET CHILD by B.J. Daniels
HI #589	THE SPECIALIST by Dani Sinclair
HI #593	THE OUTSIDER'S REDEMPTION by Joanna Wayne

Visit us at www.eHarlequin.com   HARTC

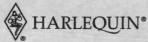

HARLEQUIN®

makes any time special—online...

eHARLEQUIN.com

your romantic life

―Romance 101―
♥ Guides to romance, dating and flirting.

―Dr. Romance―
♥ Get romance advice and tips from our expert, Dr. Romance.

―Recipes for Romance―
♥ How to plan romantic meals for you and your sweetie.

―Daily Love Dose―
♥ Tips on how to keep the romance alive every day.

―Tales from the Heart―
♥ Discuss romantic dilemmas with other members in our Tales from the Heart message board.